IN LOVE WITH AN A-TOWN THUG 2

SHANICE B.

Cole Hart
SIGNATURE HOUSE

In Love With An A-Town Thug 2

Copyright © 2019 by Shanice B.

All rights reserved.

Published in the United States of America.

Published by Cole Hart Signature, LLC.

Mailing List

To stay up to date on new releases, plus get information on contests, sneak peeks, and more,

Go To The Website Below...

WWW.COLEHARTSIGNATURE.COM

❀ Created with Vellum

SYNOPSIS

Just when Monay believes she has found love, she realizes that yet again she had been played for a fool. Monay knows deep in her heart that Jawan can't be trusted, and as much as she wants to forget him, she finds it hard to let him go.

Jawan Miles never thought that he would find himself in a position where he would have to choose between his wife, or another female. He doesn't want to lose his family, nor Monay. Working things out with Alonna would be the logical thing to do, but Jawan isn't thinking logically at all.

Alonna Miles appears to be strong, independent, and confident, but deep down she is near her breaking point. When tragedy hits close to home, both she and Jawan will have a choice to either pull together, or break free from one another. Will their marriage survive the betrayal and pain that Jawan has inflicted, or is it a little too late?

Drew Wilson is madly in love with his girlfriend Desiree, but it only takes one mistake before Drew will find himself about to lose the one girl he claimed he would always love.

In part 2 of in love with an A-Town Thug, relationships

will be tested and hearts will be broken. Will everyone get what they want in the end or will they all take an L?

ALONNA

inding out that the man I was married to was cheating on me tore me up inside, but the last thing I was going to do was let him see how much he had hurt me. I understood that Jawan and I were going to have good days and bad days when we got married, but what I didn't expect was this. Before I married Jawan, I already knew he was smashing other bitches behind my back, but the day that he put that ring on my finger, he promised me that he would never hurt me like that ever again. I believed him, I truly did. I thought he was a changed man. As the years went by, and as we both began to evolve, Jawan remained faithful and loyal to me. Until now.

Who was this bitch that he had stepped out on me with? All I knew was her name, but deep down I was far from dumb. She had to mean something to him, for him to risk our marriage. I knew deep in my soul that whatever Jawan had going on with this Monay bitch was something more then just sex.

My ego was bruised, and my heart felt like someone had taken a knife and stabbed me numerous times. I wanted to cry, but I wouldn't allow myself to be weak. Right now was not the time to be a weak bitch, it was time for me to boss up and show Jawan that he had me all the way fucked up.

I pulled up at the house that I shared with Jawan and sat in my car for the longest time. I had been so wrapped up in this pregnancy and work that I was distracted. Maybe if I would have been paying attention to Jawan and his movements, none of this would have ever happened. Monay wouldn't have ever been able to wiggle her way into my man's life. I blamed myself because when I found out I was pregnant, I lost it. This was something that Jawan wasn't expecting. I guess he thought I was going to be happy about having another baby, but when he found out that another baby wasn't what I wanted, maybe that could have caused him to shut down, and for him to look for love elsewhere.

Now that we were having marital problems, I definitely felt that this baby was coming at the wrong time.

I didn't know exactly what I was going to do about Jawan, or our marriage, but one thing I knew was for certain: him staying in this house with me wasn't about to happen. I wanted him away from me until I had a chance to cool down.

I finally stepped out of my 2018 Honda Accord a few moments later, and headed inside the house. I went straight towards our bedroom and opened his closet where he kept his clothes and shoes. I grabbed everything that was hanging up in his closet and threw them onto our bed. When all of his clothes had been taken out, I started on his shoes throwing them into a pile on the floor. It took me nearly an hour for me to empty his closet. I didn't want shit in my house that belonged to him. Right now, I wanted to erase him from my life until I was ready to deal with the issue. I have never been the type of bitch who let her emotions get the best of her, but when I reached the bathroom and spotted some Clorox near the bathtub, an idea quickly came to me.

I had so much going for myself. I was educated and independent. I made my own money, and never asked him for shit. For him to even want to cheat on me let me knew that he was one dumb ass nigga.

I headed back to my bedroom and grabbed as many clothes that I could carry and shoved them into the bathtub. I grabbed the clorox that was on the floor and started pouring them over everything in the tub. When the clothes were drenched, I went back in the bedroom, grabbed more clothes and shoes and bleached them bitches, too. I was just about to bleach more of his shoes when I heard Jawan yell out my name.

I froze. Not out of fear, but because I wasn't ready to see him. I had planned on coming home and throwing all his clothes out of the window to our bedroom, but then I got distracted by the clorox and decided, *"why throw his clothes out the window when I could destroy them?"*

He had money. He could go buy himself new clothes and shoes. I just wanted to fuck some shit up ,and the fact that I couldn't fight his ass and actually win, bleaching his clothes would suffice.

Most women would have went after the bitch for fucking their man in the first place. The only reason why I didn't take that route was because I knew that one day, I was going to catch that bitch alone, and when I did, I was going to wear that ass out. The only thing that stopped me from jumping on her when I spotted her with Jawan, was because she had no clue that the bastard was married. Apparently, he had been lying to her ass, and she was too young and naive to see through his bullshit.

"Alonna, what the fuck are you doing, and why the hell does it smells like bleach in here?!" Jawan yelled out as he made his way into our bedroom.

I stood up from the tub that I had been bent over and

waited for him to come into the bathroom. A few seconds later, he walked in and all hell broke loose when he saw what I was doing.

"What the fuck is wrong with you? You actually bleached my fucking clothes and shoes? Bitch, have you lost your fucking mind?" he asked me furiously.

I should have been scared, but baby, the rage that I was feeling inside of me was finally about to be set free. If he thought he was going to talk shit to me, he had another thing coming. I was ready to get straight donkey stupid on his lying ass.

"Nigga, the last thing you need to be worried about are these clothes. You can buy new clothes, but you can't buy another life. You need to be worried about what I'm willing to do to your stupid ass for cheating on me with that little bitch."

"Alonna, you ain't going to do shit," he spat at me.

"You don't know me at all if you think I'm going to be one of these stupid ass hoes running around here, married to a street thug who has multiple bitches they fucking on. That ain't me bruh. You're married to the wrong one if you think I'm about to stay with you after this."

I tried to leave out the bathroom but he grabbed me by my arm and told me that I wasn't going anywhere until we talked things out.

"Let me fucking go. I want you out of this house. I need my space to think and I don't want you around me," I replied furiously.

"This is my damn house. I ain't going nowhere, just let me explain please."

"I don't want to hear your sorry ass story. I know what you were doing at that condo. Matter of fact, I ain't even know about the condo until I tracked your phone to that location. You been hiding a lot of shit from me lately. I don't know what I was thinking when I married you, but if I could go back in time, I wouldn't have ever said, *'I Do'* to your lying ass. Once a cheater, always a cheater," I spat at him nastily.

I tried yanking my arm out of Jawan's grasp, but he held on to me tightly.

"Look, if you don't fucking let me go, I swear I will kill your ass. I will gladly do life in prison. At least then, I will know that you will never have me looking stupid again."

"Look, shut the fuck up and stop making threats," he demanded.

When he finally let me go, I pushed past him, headed into our bedroom, and grabbed the little bit of clothes he had that were still lying on the bed. I was headed to the window when he told me to leave his shit alone.

I was a hard headed bitch, and when I was pissed I could be evil as hell. I ignored his comments and continued to my destination, only for him to push me up against the wall. He shoved me so hard, I felt like my breath had been knocked out of my body. As soon as I got the opportunity, I swung at him and hit him in the face. He grunted in pain and rubbed his hand on the side I'd just struck him on.

I saw the anger in his eyes and I knew he was about to snatch my ass up, but I wasn't having that shit. I wasted no time kicking him between his legs, which brought him down to eye level with me. I spit in his face and punched him with so much force that he fell to the floor.

Jawan was over six-five and strong; he could have easily beat my ass, but I guess he knew if he hit me back that was only going to make shit worse. He knew deep down he deserved the blows that I had just delivered. I had asked him to leave, he didn't want to, so an ass whooping it was going to be. I grabbed the clothes that had fallen to the floor during our struggle and threw them out the window.

"Why won't you listen to me?" Jawan asked as he picked himself up off the floor.

"Because I know what you are about to say is a whole bunch of bullshit."

"It's not bullshit. Look, I'm sorry for cheating on you, but I didn't actually fuck her. I haven't been in the streets trying to find someone to fuck, if that's what you thinking."

"Nigga, get the fuck out of my house. You ain't sorry, but you soon will be, if you don't leave me the hell alone. Take your ass back to that little young bitch you was laid up with. What we had is over with. We're done bruh. You don' fucked everything up. The little love I had for you is gone. So get the little shit you do have left, and bounce."

"You need to calm your ass down, Alonna. Think about the baby."

"The baby? Oh, so now you want to bring the baby up in this conversation. If you're so concerned about the baby, you wouldn't have done anything to jeopardize my sanity. Your ass wouldn't have been out trying to get some new pussy if you actually cared about this baby's well being. I didn't want this baby before, and I damn sure don't want the baby now that we ain't together anymore!" I screamed at him.

I could see the rage in Jawan's face, but I didn't give a fuck. How dare he get me pregnant, when he knew I wanted to pursue my career? How dare he cheat on me and have me raising three kids on my own? I swear, I was ready to make his life hell if it came to that. If he had any sense, he would end things with Monay.

I was just about to say some more shit to him, but I was cut short when he grabbed me by my neck and choked me out. He shoved me up against the wall as my feet dangled in the air.

"I've told you to watch your mouth when it comes to that baby that you're carrying. Now, I have told you that I'm sorry for talking to someone, so let the shit go. I'm trying to be the bigger person and talk things out, but you don't want to listen. I never said I was leaving you," he spat at me.

The entire time that he was talking I was kicking and trying to catch some air in my lungs. I felt like I was going to pass out if he didn't let me go soon. I didn't want to give up the fight but I was beginning to feel weak. Was this nigga about to choke me to death? Was I going to die today? If I did, then maybe it wasn't such a bad thing. Maybe then I would be free and not have to worry anymore.

I wanted to be free. I didn't want to be tied down to anyone or anything. Instead of fearing death, I began to embrace it. Just when I was about to close my eyes and fall into a deep sleep, Jawan released his death grip on me, and I fell down on my knees gasping for air.

I let my lungs take as much air in as I could before I finally stood up on shaky legs and screamed at Jawan to get out. He must have been shaken himself, since he nearly killed my ass. I was grateful when he finally listened to me and left. I waited until I heard the front door close before I fell back down onto the floor, and finally let out the tears that I had been holding back since spotting him with some other chick.

I never cried, but today, I had to shed tears for my own sanity. I wasn't crying because I was sad. I was crying because the man I loved with all my heart had just turned me ice cold. Rage filled my soul and I wanted him to hurt like he had hurt me. The only way to bring that nigga to his knees was for me to leave him for good.

ALONNA

The Next Day

*T*he last thing I wanted to do was go to work, but lying in bed all day wasn't going to make me any money. I needed to get as much money as I could because I was going to need it to be able to support myself and the kids. I rolled out of bed and slowly walked towards my bathroom so I could take care of my hygiene. When I stared into the bathroom mirror, the reflection I saw was of a woman who had been broken. My once vibrant, light toned features now looked pale. I was definitely going to have to wear some type of makeup to bring some life to my complexion.

My eyes were swollen from crying and my hair looked a mess. My heart felt as if a ton of weights were sitting on top of my chest. All I could think about was Jawan betraying me. I thought we had something good, but maybe it was I who was living in a delusional mindset. Maybe our relationship had been over, and it was me who didn't see it coming.

I hopped in the shower and took care of my business. As I scrubbed myself clean, I tried thinking of what I was going to do next with my life. I was definitely going to need help with the kids if I really planned on leaving Jawan alone. Most women would stay and settle with their man having another bitch on the side, but I wasn't cut from that type of cloth. Either he was with me, or I was single. It wasn't about to be a three way triangle in this relationship.

After I washed myself clean, I stepped out of the shower and wrapped a towel around my wet body. I headed to my room and hurried to find a pair of scrubs to wear to work because I was running behind. I decided on a pair of grey scrubs with my black and grey Nike tennis shoes. After putting on my clothes, I headed back to the bathroom so I could try to put a little makeup on my face.

After dabbing on a little powder and eyeliner, I made sure to finger comb my short hair. Once I was satisfied with my appearance, I grabbed my purse from off my bed and headed out to start my day.

I arrived at Northside hospital and tried to avoid socializing. I wasn't in the mood to talk to anyone. I just wanted to do my job so I could go home and decide what I was going to do with my life. Every time one of my coworkers would come up to me wanting to chit-chat, I ignored them, and they would get the hint and leave me the hell alone. The technique was working just fine until it was time for my lunch break. I headed to the cafeteria to get something to eat, when I bumped into Dr. Cordan Williams.

"Do you want to have lunch together today?" Dr. Williams asked.

"I'm not in the mood for talking," I responded dryly before walking past him into the cafeteria and paying for my food.

Just when I thought Cordan had caught the hint and would leave me alone, he came up and took a seat in front of me at the lunchroom table.

I stared at him oddly and he flashed me a sexy smile which made my heart skip a beat. Even though I was angry and didn't want to be bothered with anybody, it was something about Cordan that wanted me to make him an exception to the game.

"You aren't acting like yourself. Is everything okay?" Cordan asked concerned.

"Yes, everything is fine," I responded irritably.

No matter how hard I tried to avoid noticing Cordan, I still found myself lusting after him in my head. Today wasn't the day to have any lustful thoughts though. I wanted him to leave me alone, but Cordan had other plans.

We ate in silence which I was cool with, but I should have known he was only thinking up ways on how he was going to get me to open up to him, and actually make me communicate.

"I know that look all too well."

"What look?" I asked with confusion laced in my tone.

"You've got that empty look in your eyes," he replied.

"I don't want to talk about it," I responded coldly.

"Look, I'm not trying to pressure you to talk to me about your personal life, I'm just saying, whatever you're going through, you don't have to deal with it alone. I'm here to listen if you ever want to talk," Cordan stated seriously.

I swallowed the last bit of my drink and stood up so I could dump my trash.

"Holding all that anger inside is only going to make it worse. You will find yourself living in hell, if you don't get yourself together and get out of your head."

I gave him a fake smile.

"Cordan, do me a favor and stop being so fucking thirsty." I walked away before he was able to say anything in response.

I needed to get away from him. The fact that I was very

attracted to him wasn't helping me in my situation. I wanted to have a clear level head and spilling my pain out to a man who resembled Idris Elba wasn't going to get me any closer to fixing my marriage. It would only destroy the little bit that I had treasured in my heart. I knew Dr. Cordan Williams wanted more than just a friendship. I was far from dumb; I saw how he looked at me every chance he got.

Fucking another man to get over another one always seemed to help in situations like these, but, at the end of the day, I was still married *and* pregnant. I was tempted every day by Cordan, but I wasn't about to fall victim to the temptation and the sexual energy he was giving off.

As soon as I stepped out of the cafeteria, my breathing finally returned to normal. Cordan was a big flirt, but maybe he didn't deserve the cold shoulder that I had just given him. Maybe he was really concerned for my mental state, or he could be like some of these other niggas who would do and say anything to hit.

As I headed back to finish my rounds for that day, I couldn't help but ponder on the warning he had given me about living in my head. Whether he knew it or not, I was already living in my own hell inside of my head.

Later That Day

After getting off of work, I headed to my parents' house so I could pick up my kids. Lately, my mama had been kind enough to pick them up from daycare if she was getting off from work earlier than I was. Even though both my parents were career driven, they always made time for their grand-kids. My parents were lawyers, and always had a busy sched-ule, but they never let that cut in between them being grandparents. They may have cut me off financially, and were no longer giving me money, but my kids never had to suffer. I pulled up at my parents' house twenty-five minutes later, and parked beside my mama's black Murano. I stepped out of my car and knocked a few times on the front door before my mama swung it open.

"Hey Alonna, come on in sweetie. I'm making the girls some sandwiches," my mama instructed.

I walked into the house and was met by Aliana and Arianna.

"Mommmmyyy!" they screamed in union.

I got down on both knees and embraced them in a tight hug while asking them how their day had been. After talking my ear off, they ran back to the living room to finish watching their TV show. I headed into the kitchen to find my mama cutting up sandwiches. I pulled a kitchen chair out and took a seat.

"Alonna, what's bothering you? And before you lie, don't. I'm your mother, I know you."

My mama was the last person I wanted to talk about my personal problems with but if I didn't come up with something to tell her, she was only going to continue to press the issue. I blamed it on her job field. She always had questions and was nosey as hell. I guess it all came from her being a lawyer for so many years.

"I don't want to talk about it," I mumbled.

My mama scoffed.

"Oh, you're going to tell me something. You got all that heavy makeup on like you trying to hide something. I hope that husband of yours hasn't been putting his hands on you."

"No, Mama, it isn't anything like that," I told her sternly.

"Well, you could have fooled me," she muttered under her breath. "Kids, come get your sandwiches!" she yelled out next.

I heard my kids' feet as they ran into the kitchen to get

their meal. They grabbed their plates and headed back into the living room to continue watching TV.

"Ya'll better not put nothing on my couch or on that floor in there!" Mama yelled out to Aliana and Arianna.

"We won't!" my kids yelled in unison.

When Mama pulled out a chair next to me at the table, I knew we were about to have a mother-daughter talk, which I hated.

"Baby, I know that we haven't always gotten along, but I hate that you feel like you can't come talk to me about things when you are having issues."

I sighed.

The only reason why Mama and I weren't close was because she was too judgmental. If I didn't do it *her* way, then I was automatically going in the wrong direction or doing things incorrectly.

Things haven't been right between me and Mama since I went and married Jawan. She had told me that he wasn't the man for me. I hated to admit the shit, but maybe Mama was right. Jawan and I were two different people who wanted different things out of life. Back then, I thought love would conquer all. Now, I knew that was all bullshit.

"Mom, every time I try talking to you about anything, you always criticize and judge me, which is why I keep things to myself."

"Baby, I'm sorry if you feel that way, but I only want the best for you. You are my only child. I just want you to be happy with life and looking at you right now, I can tell that you are far from being happy. Just open up and talk to me, maybe I can help."

I shook my head.

"There's nothing you can do Mama. It's too late."

She grabbed me by my hands and told me to look at her. I

stared into her deep brown eyes as she told me how sorry she was for pushing me away.

"I know things have been crazy between us since you decided to get married ten years ago, but I miss us. I miss how things used to be before you decided to get married. I know you're grown and are able to make your own decisions. I'm sorry if I appear overbearing. I can't help it. I don't want you or my grandbabies to suffer if you don't have to. I was showing you tough love when I cut you off financially, but now, your father and I have come to realize that tough love only pushed you further away from us. "

When I saw tears forming in her eyes, I knew that she meant every word that she had just said. My mama never cried, so I knew it took everything out of her to express her true feelings towards me.

I took a deep breath and decided to tell her everything. If she could open up to me and show me her weakness, then I was willing to do the same.

"Jawan is cheating on me," I muttered softly.

"Awww baby, do you know who the girl is?"

"No, I don't know her personally, but I have met her. Jawan was supposed to have met me at the doctor's office for a check up about the baby, but I couldn't get in touch with him so I tracked his phone and went to the address. Turns out, it was a condo that I didn't even know about. The female is younger than me, and she seemed clueless. She didn't even know he was married."

My mama didn't speak for the longest time. Instead, she embraced me in a tight hug, and told me that she was there for me if I needed her. Tears fell down my cheeks as I cried.

I pulled away from her a few moments later, and she wiped the tears from her eyes.

"I just don't know what to do Mama. I put him out, but deep down I still miss him. I'm just angry that he would do something like this to us. We have never cheated on one another, so for him to step out I'm beginning to wonder if he loves her."

"Sweetie, try to calm down. Everything is going to be okay. If you need me or your father, we're here. You're married. I can't tell you what to do about your marriage, only you can do that. All I can tell you is to find out the truth. Find out what type of relationship that your husband has with this other female, and once you know that, you will know what to do next. Nobody is perfect. We all fuck up. The only thing you can do is pull yourself together and talk to him about it. Ask him all the hard questions, and be prepared to emotionally and mentally deal with the answers."

"Thanks Mama, for listening."

"Of course, sweetie."

I stood up and told her that I had to go and see if I could talk to Jawan. My mama told me that she was willing to keep the kids until I got everything figured out with our marriage.

"These kids are young. They should stay here with me and your father, until you and Jawan have gotten everything taken care of. I don't want them witnessing the arguing. You need some time to yourself to get yourself together emotionally."

"Thanks Mama, for everything."

"You're welcome, baby."

I hugged and kissed my two girls goodbye and told them that they were going to be staying with their granny for a little while longer. The girls didn't even budge; they were engrossed in their TV show.

"Be strong baby girl," my mama instructed.

"I will."

I waved bye, walked out of her house, and headed to my car.

As soon as I slid into my Honda, I pulled out my phone to hit Jawan up. He picked up on the first ring.

"Baby?"

"Don't baby me. Meet me at the house. I'm ready to talk," I instructed him.

I pulled up at our house fifteen minutes later. He was already there waiting on me. I parked next to him and stepped out my car. He hopped out of his all black F150 truck, and walked over to where I stood.

"Alonna, I just want to apologize for hurting you and breaking your heart. I know we have been having a hard time lately, but we are going to get through this."

I listened as he continued to tell me how sorry he was, and how he didn't want to lose me. It was comical to me at first, but I could hear my mama in my head telling me to shut his ass up and ask all the hard questions that I was scared to ask.

I held my hand up to let Jawan know that his time was up for talking.

"I heard everything you said, and all of that is sweet and all, but it's meaningless until you answer this one question. Do you love this Monay bitch?"

Jawan became speechless, and he couldn't even look me in the face. I knew then that it was too late; I had already lost him.

MONAY

*T*his had to be a nightmare. This couldn't be true. I couldn't believe that I had been made a fool of. As tears rolled down my cheeks, I couldn't help but wonder how long it was going to take me to get myself back together. First Drew, and now Jawan. Falling in love with a street thug always left me broken hearted, and I was getting sick of being played for a sucker. Jawan had been blowing up my phone non stop, but not once had I answered or responded to any of his text messages. Most females would have blocked his ass, but not me.

I still had so much love for him, and just the thought of never hearing from him again, tore me up inside. I honestly believed in my heart, that maybe Jawan was the one who had come in my life to save me. I thought he was going to be the one to love me and do things for me that no other man has ever done, but he was like all the others. He had lied and betrayed me as well.

I never could understand how a man could stare a bitch in her face and lie without feeling any guilt. I believe that a person who could do that, didn't have a heart or soul.

Learning that the man that I had fallen for so easily, without even giving it a second thought ,was married, and that hurt the most. Why didn't he tell me? Why did he keep that a secret? I couldn't wrap my head around any of it. Not only did he lie about being married, this nigga lied about having kids, too. Just thinking about what he had done made me cry harder.

When I saw that bitch get out of her car when Jawan and I were about to leave his condo that day, I thought she was some random hoe that he used to kick it with. I was ready to go to war over his ass and fight for what I wanted, but when that bitch told me that she was his wife, and was pregnant with his third child, I felt like I had been punched in the face. There was no fighting involved. Just the sight of her was enough to know that I didn't have any ownership of this man.

He was just a nigga who had eaten my pussy. The thought of being a side piece made me sick to my stomach. I hadn't made it hard for Jawan to squeeze his way into my life. I left the door wide open by being vulnerable after going through the betrayal of my best friend, Desiree, sleeping with my boyfriend, Drew. I wasn't quite yet over that shit, then Jawan came, saying all the right things. I fell for his charm when I should have been cautious. This was another lesson learned. I was tired of getting fucked over. I was beginning to just say 'fuck all men', and just focus on myself for a while. What was the point in falling in love, when all they did was stab you in the back once they got a chance?

I wiped the tears from my eyes and hurried to the bathroom to wash my face once I heard my mama calling out for me. My mama was finally back home from the hospital, but she wasn't doing any better. She had only been home for a day, and the entire time, she constantly cried about being in pain. My heart broke for her, and I hated to see her in this condition.

Right now, my mama needed me and I was going to do my part in taking care of her. Some daughters wouldn't have lifted a finger, but what me and my mama had gone through was now in the past. After she stopped doing drugs and started to try to change her life around, I released all the hate and anger that I had built up in my heart for her. All I had now for my mama was love, and she also had the same for me.

After washing my face, I headed into my mama's room to find her trying to get out of bed.

In her mind, my mama thought she was able to still go about her day like she used to, but the cancer had spread very quickly and her movements were limited.

The fact that Mama never went to the doctor, and was so heavily on drugs, she had prevented herself from being diagnosed with cancer early on. Being told that she only had six months to live kilted my mama; the only thing she wanted to do was come home and be in her own home.

Even though I was tired from working a full shift last night, I knew my mama needed me.

"Mama, why didn't you wait for me to come help you? You're way too weak; I don't want you to fall."

"Monay, I don't want to hear what I can't do. I can take myself to the damn bathroom, girl."

I shook my head as I walked over to where she was and helped guide her to the bathroom.

"I swear ,since you found out I had cancer you've been babying me, like I'm some infant," she muttered under breath.

"I know you're upset Mama, but that's the point of you coming home, so that I can take care of you. I could have easily signed you into a home," I told her sternly.

"I rather be home with you," she admitted.

Since I had been in this world, I never saw her so weak, frail, and broken. I helped her down on the toilet even though she didn't want me to.

"Either you're going to let me help you, or I will apply for a CNA to come take care of you."

"No, I'd rather have you," Mama replied quietly.

"Good."

After my mom used the bathroom, I ran her some water in the tub so she could bathe. I listened to her fuss about how she could do all things by herself.

Once she was all cleaned from her bath, and after I brushed what little hair she had left on her head, I laid her down in her queen sized bed.

"Do you want the TV on?" I asked as I grabbed the remote off of her nightstand.

"No, I don't want to watch TV. I want to talk to you. Sit down for a minute."

"What do you want to talk about?" I questioned as I took a seat next to her.

"What's going on with you? You look like shit, and I'm the one who is supposed to be sick."

I chuckled.

"You ain't too sick, you're still talking shit."

My mama laughed.

"Oh, I'm just stating facts. I'm your mama, I know when something is up with you, and you look like you've been crying."

"I'm fine mama, don't worry about me. I can handle myself," I told her as I stood up to leave.

"Sit back down, Monay, and talk to me. I'm trying to be here for you and make our relationship stronger, I know it's probably a little too late, but let me give you some motherly love."

I saw the tears starting to form in her eyes and I sighed.

"Mama, it's not too late. As long as you have air in your lungs, anything can be fixed."

Mama nodded her head as she waited on me to tell her what was really bothering me.

I bit down on my bottom lip and took a deep breath.

"Remember the dude you met at the hospital? The one you liked."

"You mean Jawan?" My mama asked.

I smiled weakly.

"I can't believe you remembered his name."

"Yes, I can't forget him. How he talked about you to me, I knew he was the one for you."

"I thought so too, but looks like we both were wrong."

My mama scoffed.

"I'm a lot of things but I'm a good judge of character."

"Sorry Mama, but I think you had him all wrong."

"What happened Monay?"

I didn't want to cry. I really didn't, but every time I thought about how things went down I always found myself crying my eyes out. I took a deep breath before telling her everything.

"I was made a complete fool of. He wasn't who he appeared to be. Turns out he's married, with two kids, and one on the way with his wife."

My mama grew silent. For the first time she was speechless.

"Don't you have anything to say?" I asked her as the tears poured down my face.

My mama looked over at me and gave me a weak smile.

"Sometimes men do stupid shit baby. We're all human, but if he lied to you about his wife and kids, then I suggest you be cautious of him."

"No worries, I cut his ass off. I've been avoiding him."

"You can't avoid him forever. Eventually you're going to have to sit down and talk to this man to get things straight. I know you're angry, and I know you may feel like he played you, but baby, when he talked about how much he cared about you when I was in that hospital bed, I knew that he was different. I felt that shit in my soul, and I saw it in his eyes. One thing I do know, a man's eyes do not lie. It's the gateway to their very soul. That man does care and love you, but maybe he has some shit that he has to get settled. Who knows, but just know if I were you, I would give him a chance to at least explain himself."

By this time, my entire body was shaking and I was crying silently. My mama grabbed me by my arm and held me to her chest.

"Baby, sometimes we find ourselves in situations that we never thought we would be in. You can't help who you love, and you can't help who loves you. I know you're still raw inside from what Drew and Desiree did, but Jawan isn't Drew; he's different. I can't really put my finger on it, but the love he has is a different type of love that Drew had for you. What Drew had for you was fake love, until he found something better, but what Jawan has for you is so much more than that. Talk with him, sweetie. Find out his side of the story. Find out why he lied. Get to the bottom of it, and then decide for yourself what you want to do."

"I just feel like he didn't let me make my own choice when it came to us talking. He should have been upfront with me, from jump."

"Yes, he should have, but every man is different and they all handle things differently when it comes to getting to know someone they potentially want to become serious with, especially if they feel it will jeopardize the relationship."

My mama wiped the tears from my eyes, and for the first time, comforted me through my heart break.

As she held me to her chest, I decided to close my eyes. My soul was finally at peace. Just knowing my mama was there with me made the pain tolerable, but my heart was still broken.

MONAY

Later That Day…

I had just finished getting dressed for work, when I headed to my mother's bedroom to find her lying in bed half asleep, watching TV. The only time I left her alone was when I had to go to work at night. I still hated to leave her by herself, but I didn't have a choice. I couldn't miss work and I didn't know anyone that could watch over her until I got back.

This was going to be the second night that I had to work. The night before, Mama stayed sleep the entire night and didn't wake up until early this morning. Hopefully, tonight there wouldn't be any problems, either.

I walked over to my mama's bed to let her know that I was about to leave for the night.

"Be careful sweetie," she said sleepily.

"I will be safe, I promise," I whispered to her before bending down and placing a kiss on her forehead.

"Try not to get out this bed if you don't have to. I hate to leave you here by yourself, but I don't have anyone else that I can call. Your homegirl Judy is in drug rehab, and she isn't going to get back into a few days."

"Go to work, Monay. I'm not leaving this bed."

"Have a good night Mama; if you need me call me."

After leaving out of Mama's room, I grabbed the keys to my car and headed out of the house. I hopped in my car and was just about to pull off when a black truck swooped in and blocked me in. I looked in my rearview mirror and groaned when I spotted Jawan getting out of his truck.

I stepped out and walked over to him.

"What in the hell are you doing here? You're going to have me late for work," I told him crossly.

"I've been calling and texting but you won't pick up," he explained.

"Maybe because I don't have shit to say to you," I replied with attitude.

"Please, Monay, just let me explain," Jawan begged.

Even though I was pissed and angry, I was more hurt than anything, so I decided to let him explain. I wanted to know why he lied to me anyway.

"Explain yourself and don't take all day because I got to get to work."

"Monay, I'm sorry for lying to you. When you first asked me if I was single or had kids, I told you no because at that time I did feel single. Me and the wife were having issues, and still are, but that didn't give me an excuse to lie. You're innocent and so sweet and loving. I knew if I would have come clean and told you that I was married with two kids and one on the way, you wouldn't have given me a second. You wouldn't even have let me get to know you because you would have automatically thought there could never be an us. I know you ain't into the side chick shit, and just to be clear, I don't want a side chick anyway. I eventually was going to tell you about my wife and kids, but I didn't know that you were going to find out before I actually sat you down and tried to talk to you about it."

He was about to say more but I smacked the shit out of his ass.

"That was fucked up of you. You didn't give me a choice. You made it for me! I fell in love with you based on the lies that you told me!" I shouted at him.

"Baby, calm down please."

"Don't baby me. Why are you even here? Shouldn't you be with your wife, seeing about your kids, and trying to fix shit with her?" I asked him angrily.

Jawan began walking towards me and I took a few steps back until I hit the back of my car. There was no where else for me to go and he knew that. He closed the distance between us. His cologne filled my nose, and he was looking so damn fine. If we wouldn't have been on bad terms, I would have ran into his arms and kissed him.

When he rubbed his fingers against my cheek, I wanted to pull away but I couldn't. He stared down at me and I saw tears forming in his eyes.

A street nigga crying? Damn, I never thought I would ever see some shit like this.

"I can't stop thinking about you. I know we haven't been talking long before all this shit blew up, and all the lies coming out, but I can't walk away from what we could have. Do you still care about a nigga or do you hate me?"

"I don't hate you Jawan. I'm angry and upset you lied to me. You had me thinking it could be an us and that's never going to happen, because you already belong to someone," I stated weakly.

I was near tears; we both were. Both of our emotions were raw. I didn't want to lose him, but I didn't want to share him, either.

"We can still be together baby. Me being married doesn't change anything."

"It changes *everything* Jawan. I'm not settling for being someone you fuck on whenever you feel like it."

"No, you mean more to me than just some easy pussy. I want you to be mine."

"How can I be yours? Explain that shit to me, Jawan. Make this shit make sense."

Jawan took a few steps back as he rubbed his hand through his freshly twisted dreads.

"We can make it happen baby. Just hang tight."

I shook my head at him. It was time for me to be a woman and ask him the one question that was burning in my mind. I didn't know exactly what answer I was going to get but I wanted to know. Was I wasting my time loving a man who was never going to be mine?

"You came all the way to my house to confess your love to me and to apologize, but you ain't told me the one thing I want to know."

"What do you want to know?" Jawan asked.

"Are you going to leave your wife and actually be with me?"

Jawan became silent.

I didn't dare take my eyes off of him, I wanted to know exactly what he was planning on doing.

"Baby, I don't want to lie to you."

"Then don't lie; for once, be real with me."

"I promise that we are going to be together soon, but I just need a little more time to handle things with my wife."

"Your time is up, I have to head to work," I said before I headed back.

"Monay, I love you."

"Of course you do," I muttered under my breath before stepping back into my car.

I waited until he moved his truck and that's when I pulled out and headed to work. The entire ride, all I could think about was Jawan and what he said. He promised me that we were going to be together, but was he lying? Was he just telling me that so he wouldn't lose me? Was he planning on trying to keep me and his wife? I was stressed, no doubt, as I tried to figure out what I was going to do next.

I pulled up fifteen minutes later and hopped out. I wasn't working alone tonight. Jasele was there and she was already on the phone talking with a customer. I clocked in and as soon as I was about to have a seat behind the counter, the phone began to ring. I picked up and booked a few rooms before everything grew silent.

"Damn boo, what's up with you?" Jasele asked, after I booked the last room.

"Ugh, I don't even want to talk about it," I mumbled.

"Well sometimes, you have to get it out and talk to some-one. You can trust me. I'm not going to tell your business to anyone. Shit, I don't even have any friends to talk to myself."

I shook my head.

Trusting people was why I kept getting fucked over in the first place. Not everyone could be trusted. But the only reason why I even opened my mouth to tell Jasele anything, was because she always had married men after her. It all had to do with her looks and the fact that she had a body like a model. I knew for a fact she was all too familiar on what to do about my situation, or better yet, how to handle it.

"Since me and you have been working together, I've noticed a lot of men who are married have tried getting with you. I just need a little advice on that topic."

"Okay, I will tell you anything you want to know."

"I was talking to someone and I was really feeling them, but then I found out that he's married with kids. I mean, I just feel so lost right now. He says that he wants to be with me, but he needs time to get things squared away with his wife. I don't even know if I should trust him."

Jasele stopped typing on her computer and gave me her full attention.

"Do you want my honest opinion on what you should do? Never mind, let me tell you this story about a friend that I used to know some years back."

"Okayyyyy, cool. If you think it's going to help me with my situation."

"Yeah, I believe it will help lead you in the right direction."

"My friend, she fell in love with this married man once. She knew he was married when they first met, so she knew what she was getting herself into. He told her that he was going to leave his wife and be with her, but it never happened. Eventually, my friend found out that he was lying to her the entire time. He wanted to keep her for his side chick and continue to stay married to his wife. She finally left him when she spotted him with his wife one day coming out of the grocery store. His wife was heavily pregnant which my friend automatically knew belonged to her boyfriend. The sad part was, he walked right past my friend and acted like he didn't even know her."

I shook my head.

"Damn, I know your friend was hurt."

"Yes, she was. She nearly lost her mind after that. It took her nearly two years for her to get her life back on track. All I'm saying is, be careful with your heart. I wouldn't want to wish that pain on anyone."

Jasele and I worked the remainder of our shift in silence. She was busy filling out applications for her modeling gigs and I was in deep thought about my love life. When it was time for us to clock out, I hurried to grab my things so I could head home to see about my mama.

Just when I was about to leave, Jasele grabbed me by my arm and embraced me in a hug.

"That story that I was telling you about earlier," Jasele stated quietly.

"Yeah what about it?"

"I left out a big detail."

"What do you mean?" I asked curiously.

"The girl who I said was a friend of mine, was actually me. I was the one who fell in love with a married man and ended up getting broken hearted. I don't want you to make the same mistake. You have a good heart, and have always been good to me since I've been working here. You don't deserve that type of pain."

I stood there in utter disbelief as Jasele grabbed her things and headed out the double doors. I left a few moments later, and the last thing I was expecting to see was Jawan waiting outside next to my car.

"Why are you here?" I asked.

"I came to see you," he replied.

He walked over to me and pulled me into his arms. I should have pulled away, but I didn't. Even though I knew that loving this man would lead me to being hurt, I still couldn't find the strength to give him up.

"I love you girl. I'm never leaving you," he whispered into my ear.

I closed my eyes as I snuggled deeper into his chest. I felt safe and loved when I was near him. I was addicted to him and I didn't want to leave Jawan even though I knew he could be bad for me. I prayed that this time Jawan wasn't lying or keeping secrets. Maybe he did love me and was going to eventually leave his wife. *But what if he didn't leave, then what?* The voice in my head asked. If he was lying, then I needed to be preparing myself for the pain that I was going to soon be faced with.

JAWAN

I always said that I would never cheat on my wife with another female, but Monay had come into my life and changed all that shit. The crazy part about the shit, was that me and Monay haven't even had sex yet. I had just eaten her pussy and that was it. I would have given her the pipe, but Alonna showed up and fucked everything up.

I wasn't with Monay because of the sex, though. I fell in love with Monay because of her mind and her personality. I still loved my wife, but I wanted Monay, too. I knew that I couldn't have them both and I didn't want to have to choose. I had been with my wife since high school and we had kids together. I just recently met Monay and she had already came in and turned my world upside down.

I couldn't just let Monay go, no matter how much I knew I was going to have to, if I was going to try and work things out with my wife. Alonna had every right to be pissed and salty with me. I had fucked up and broken my promise to never hurt her again. I knew my wife very well. She would act tough because she didn't want me to see her hurt, but deep down I knew her soul was in turmoil.

I hated myself for hurting her, but it wasn't intentionally. It was something about Monay that made me question everything that I had with Alonna. When I was around Monay, I felt as if I had married the wrong woman. My heart was split into two, and I didn't know what to do.

Since I found out about Alonna being pregnant, so much had changed. Even Alonna had changed. I felt she wasn't the same woman that I married. After learning she didn't even want our baby, it really made me side eye her ass. During my moment of weakness, I had turned to Monay. I fell in love with her innocence and no matter how much I wanted her, I already knew I wasn't going to be able to please them both.

I wanted to be selfish and hold on to Monay until I no longer could. I didn't want another nigga to get her because if they ever did, I knew she would forget about me and go on and live her life.

Some would call me a fuck nigga for the games I was playing between these two women, but I didn't consider myself that. I was just a typical ass nigga who was in love with more than one female. The first thing I needed to do was try to get Alonna's mind and emotions back on track. She was suffering inside, and it was all because of my dumb ass. I didn't want all of this negativity to have a bad effect on our baby.

I grabbed my phone from off of the passenger seat and decided to call my wife. When I heard her voice over the phone, I couldn't help but smile. I began to think about the old days when we first fell in love.

"What are you doing tonight? Do you have any plans?" I asked quizzically.

"Why are you asking?" Alonna questioned curiously.

"If you don't have any plans, I was wondering if you would like to go out to dinner so we can talk."

Alonna grew quiet. At first, I thought she was going to

turn me down, but she didn't. She agreed to meet me at Olive Garden for dinner later that night. We didn't hold a conversation after agreeing to the time and location. We hung up and I placed my phone back in the passenger seat of my car. I had to run an errand before I headed over to the Olive Garden later that night, so I headed to that destination.

Fifteen minutes later, I pulled up at my neighborhood trap house to make sure everything was good. As soon as I stepped out, I spotted a few regulars who were always trying to get some crack on the low. They saw me and yelled out my name.

I nodded my head at them to let them know I saw them. They walked their skinny asses over to where I was and started complaining that something was fucked up with the new supply of crack they had just smoked. I stared at them like they were crazy.

"What you mean something wrong with the crack? I sell nothing but quality shit."

One of the crackheads shook his head at me.

"The shit you just got must be a bad batch because it didn't do shit for me," the second crackhead complained.

I looked over at the second crackhead who was complaining about the crack not get him high and shook my head at him. He was dressed in a dingy white tank top, dirty khaki shorts, and some too big, black sandals.

A female walked up a few moments later and stood behind them and started complaining about my product as well.

"That shit broke me out. I don't know what the fuck you sold us, but I want my money back," the woman stated.

She was looking a hot damn mess. Her two front teeth were missing and she was wearing clothes that were too big for her. The little hair that she did have on her head stopped at her cheekbone but it looked stringy and dirty.

All three crackheads looked at me and waited for me to answer.

"I don't give a fuck about what's wrong with either one of ya'll. Ya'll ain't about to get no damn crack refund. Yall better pop y'all a pill and get out my face."

The woman stomped off pissed but I didn't give a fuck. The two men stared me down like they were ready to box. They were talking about my product not hitting on shit, but they looked high as hell. They had to have smoked some good shit if they thought they were going to jump my ass. I stayed strapped and wasn't going to think twice about laying their asses out.

"Come on partner, lets go get a pill." The nigga with the dingy white tank top told his friend.

"Yeah, ya'll better do that shit," I told them as they walked off. Druggies were always trying to get over on us dope boys, but they weren't about to get over on me today. I headed into the trap house and dapped up a few of the young niggas that were living in the neighborhood. I checked the paperwork to make sure that the money, dope, and guns were where they needed to be.

After I saw that everything was good, I dipped out. I never stayed at the trap house too long. I was paranoid as hell when it came to the law. Them niggas thought they were smart, but I knew what was up when I spotted unmarked cars canvasing the area. They were looking for any reason to bust up in my shit, but little did they know, they could come at any time. They were never going to find my stash. That trap house they were so called watching was just a front. It was all for show to throw cops off of my trail. The trap house was just a spot where all the crackheads would come and chill at. A few of the niggas from the hood sold powder and crack but it was always small portions, never anything the feds could find if they raided my spot.

By the time I left the trap house, it was time for me to pull up at the restaurant. I was just about to send Monay a text to let her know that I was thinking about her when my phone began to ring. I picked up when I saw that it was Alonna.

"I'm here, where you at?" Alonna asked.

"I'm here as well, I'm getting out of the car. Meet me at the front entrance."

As usual, it was crowded as hell. Alonna met up with me at the door around the same time. She looked sexy in a black dress and red stilettos. She was smelling good as hell. She wore silver jewelry and her toes and nails were freshly done.

"You looking good baby," I whispered in her ear as we followed the waitress to our table.

We took a seat and went through our menu to figure out what we were going to order. Our waitress, took our drink orders and left us alone, promising to be back later to take our meal order.

I cleared my throat which got Alonna's attention.

"I'm glad you agreed to meet me tonight."

Alonna rolled her eyes.

"How are the kids doing?"

"They're with my parents for a while until we figure out what we're going to do about our marriage."

I watched her as she continued to eye her menu. She wasn't in the mood to talk. I figured she was still pissed that I never answered her question about if I was in love with Monay. If I would have told her the truth, she would hate me forever and would probably never let me see my kids again. I wanted Monay, I did, but I didn't want to lose my children in the process. I asked Alonna to join me for dinner just to see where her mind was, and to see if she even wanted to work this marriage out. If she wanted out, then I was going to have to figure out where that was going to leave me far as the kids.

The waitress came back a few moments later with our

drink orders and asked if we knew what we wanted to order. We both ordered the pasta dish. She took our menus and told us she would be back with our food shortly.

"How's the pregnancy going?" I asked Alonna.

"It's going fine. I go back to the doctor next week to see how the baby's doing."

"That's good. do you want me to come along?"

Alonna scoffed.

"Last time I told you to come along, you were too busy fucking another bitch and forgot about the appointment."

"I didn't fuck her," I hissed at Alonna.

"Jawan what we are not going to do tonight is lie. Don't lie to me, please, because I don't mind back handing your ass in this restaurant."

"I'm not lying to you, I didn't fuck her."

"If you ain't fuck her then, what in the hell she was doing at your condo? Huh, you tell me that! If you didn't fuck the bitch like you claim, then the only reason you didn't was because I popped up and spilled some tea on her ass."

I stared at her but didn't say shit.

Alonna chuckled.

"Oh, I'm sorry that I fucked up your pussy sampling time," Alonna spat angrily.

"Will you just shut the fuck up and give that shit a rest. I didn't invite you to dinner to fuss with you, I invited you here to see what we are going to do next. Are we going to make this shit work or are we going to go our separate ways?"

Alonna shook her head in disbelief.

"Whatever you got going with that other bitch, you need to end that shit."

I was just about to respond to her statement when my phone started ringing.

Alonna snatched my phone out my hand and shook her

head in disgust when she noticed that it was Monay calling me.

She threw the phone at me and got up from her chair.

"Your little bitch is calling you," Alonna hissed at me.

I tried grabbing her but she snatched her arm away from me.

"Don't make a scene," I warned her.

"Nigga, fuck you."

She was just about to leave when the waitress came back with our food.

"Is everything okay?" she asked.

"Yes, everything is fine," Alonna said tight lipped.

"Do you want me to get you a to go box?" she then asked my wife.

"Actually, that to go box would really be for my husband. I'm sure he is going to want to take his other little bitch some food once we leave here," Alonna replied.

I swear, I wanted to grab Alonna and shake her ass. She was making a fucking scene, and it was all over a phone call. I understood why she was pissed, but damn. Why couldn't she act like an adult and not like some high schooler who's feelings were hurt?

The waitress looked from me and then to my wife. She knew not to say anything else. She quickly headed to the back of the restaurant.

I was still trying to reason with Alonna but she ignored everything that I was saying to her. When she hurried out of Olive Garden, I followed behind her and called out her name to get her attention.

"Alonna, Alonna, wait. Talk to me!"

"Nah, bitch! Go talk to that hoe who just called your phone!" Alonna screamed loudly before hopping in her car and pulling out into traffic.

Having dinner with my wife wasn't supposed to turn out

like this. I wanted Alonna to forgive me so we could be in a better place, so that we could at least raise our kids in a stable home; but I highly doubted that would ever happen since Alonna was having a hard time forgiving me. The crazy thing about it all was, I really was starting to not care anymore.

ALONNA

I couldn't believe that this nigga was actually trying to play me for his fool. I was pissed off as I weaved in and out of the Atlanta traffic. What would have taken me twenty minutes to get home, only took me ten. I was surprised that the cops didn't get behind my ass. I pulled up at my crib and hopped out my car. I headed into my house and that's when shit really got real. I was in a rage and there was no calming me down. I went into my living room and started flipping shit over. I didn't give a fuck what I broke, I just needed to get my frustration and anger out some type of way.

I was dumb thinking that Jawan was going to realize that his marriage was more important to him than that bitch he was obsessing over. I was the mother of his kids, and was pregnant again by his monkey ass.

Smash! Smash! Smash!

I snatched down nearly all of our family pictures and smashed each one of them. I had a few vases that I bought for my house a few months back that I smashed to the ground without even flinching. I flipped over my coffee table, my two piece furniture set, and even threw my sixty-five inch flat screen TV to the floor. Tears fell from my eyes as I fell to the ground and cried like a newborn child. I hated that I had lost control of this situation. I was angry that another bitch had found her way into my man's heart.

Jawan and I always promised that we were always going to be together. I never thought anyone could come between us, but I had been wrong. I had gotten so comfortable in my marriage not knowing Jawan could be snatched up by another chick. I cried until I couldn't shed anymore tears and my head started throbbing. I picked myself up from the floor and wiped the snot that had fallen from my nose. I walked into my kitchen and grabbed a wine glass and mixed a drink.

I never smoked or drank alcohol on my first two pregnancies, but this pregnancy, I was stressed and was going through so much emotionally.

After pouring a drink, I went into our bathroom and dug through the bathroom closet where I knew Jawan had stashed some of his weed a while back. I grabbed the sack and headed to the bedroom so I could roll a blunt. I sat my wine glass down on my nightstand, kicked off my shoes, and got in bed. I rolled a quick joint and lit that bitch. A soon as I inhaled the fumes my mind soon began to feel at ease. I was trying to calm myself down and smoking a little weed seemed to be the only solution. When I was finished smoking, I ran a hot bath and soaked in the tub for over an hour. My phone kept going off on the bathroom counter but I ignored it and acted as if I didn't hear it. I already knew it wasn't anyone but Jawan's dumb ass calling me trying to give me a weak as apology.

I had every right to be angry. The point of it was, this Monay bitch was still calling him. That meant that he was still entertaining her, but here he was acting like he was trying to work things out for the kids' sake. Apparently, it was time for me to get my head out of the clouds and accept shit for what it was.

After stepping out of the tub, I wrapped my body into a blue towel and went into my bedroom where I found some comfortable clothes for bed. My phone continued to ring as I laid my head on my pillow. Instead of answering Jawan's calls, I decided to turn my phone completely off. I laid awake for a long time trying to imagine my life without my husband. I had been with him for so long, the feeling was foreign to me. Eventually, I dozed off and fell into a deep sleep.

* * *

I WOKE up the next morning still tired and emotionally drained. I snatched the covers off my body and headed to the bathroom to take care of my hygiene before I headed to work that morning. After brushing my teeth and finger combing my hair, I finally came up with the decision to get myself prepared to move on with my life. Forcing Jawan to choose me over this other bitch, was only going to end with one of us broken hearted. How things were looking, I seemed to be the bitch who was going to get the bad end of the stick. I held back the tears that were threatening to fall and headed back into my room to grab my phone off the bed, along with my keys, and headed out my front door.

After making it inside of my car, I powered back on my phone and waited for a few minutes as all the text messages began to come through. All of them were from Jawan. I didn't bother by answering any of them. The only thing I cared about was checking on my kids to see how they were doing with my mama. I had been so wrapped up with my life and my marriage that I hadn't even gotten the chance to reach out to them. The fact that she hadn't called let me knew that she had everything under control. After shooting a text to her, I finally pulled out into traffic and headed to work. I arrived at my job fifteen minutes later and headed inside praying that today would go by fast.

As soon as I clocked in, I immediately started doing my rounds and kept away from anyone who wanted to talk and gossip. The last thing on my mind was trying to find out who was fucking who and who was making more money than everyone else. I didn't give a fuck about any of that shit at the moment. The only thing I was trying to do, was to keep myself from losing my mind.

When it was time for my lunch, I wasn't really hungry, so I decided to skip my lunch break and sit in the break room where it was quiet. It was also where I knew no one would fuck with me. I just wanted some alone time so that I could think. I pulled out my phone when I felt a slight vibration in my pocket. I smiled when I noticed it was my mother texting me back letting me know that the kids were okay and she had just dropped them off at daycare.

I grabbed a bottle of water from the fridge and took a seat at the break room table. I popped it open and took a few sips out of it when my phone started vibrating again. I looked down and noticed that it was another message from Jawan.

My heart skipped a beat as I finally gained the courage to see exactly what he was talking about. I read at least fifteen of his texts before I placed my phone back into my scrub pockets. I was near tears as Jawan tried to apologize about dinner last night, but it wasn't anything that he could say or do to make me feel better about the situation.

When Jawan cheated on me, that took something out of me. He destroyed the love that we shared. What I expected him to do after he fucked up was block her ass and stop dealing with her. It was common sense to block any bitch you had feelings or relations with if they were going to cause an issue in our marriage. I shouldn't have to tell him this shit, he should know how to do it on his own. The fact that he didn't is what tore me up inside. Did he not love me enough? What had I done so fucking bad that he would hurt me in this way? No matter how hard I tried to forget about what Jawan had done, it still invaded my brain. No matter how hard I tried to think of other things, Jawan always managed to resurface in my thoughts. I had kids with this man. He was always going to be a fixture in my life. I honestly didn't know how I was going to be able to detach myself and move on with my life knowing that he was always going to be a part of it in some way.

The pain from the heartache and the raw feelings that I was trying to cover up resurfaced and tears began to fall from my eyes. I was so deep into my feelings that I didn't even hear anyone coming up from behind me until I felt someone touch me lightly on my shoulder.

"Shhhh, don't cry beautiful."

I didn't even have to turn around to realize that it was Dr. Cordan Williams.

"What's wrong? Why are you so upset?" Cordan asked with concern.

I hurried to try and wipe the tears from my eyes as Cordan took a seat next to me.

"I have never seen you this upset. Talk to me Alonna, I'm here for you if you need me."

Whether Doctor Williams knew it or not, he was the last person I wanted to talk to. I have never appeared weak in front of a man and here he was, with this sympathetic look on his face. I hated the feeling and wanted to get away from him. He must have known from my facial expression that he was the last person who I would open up to.

"Alonna, I know I may have been coming on to you too strongly lately. I'm sorry that it has made you feel uncomfortable. If you would just take the time to get to know me, you would find out that I'm not who you think I am. I'm a very good man; it's just that once I get fixated on something or someone, that person or thing is all I can think about. In this case, I'm fixated on you; getting to know you, trying to persuade you to let me into your world. I respect your marriage. I just want you to know that I'm not trying to be disrespectful to you."

I listened but never responded. I was too busy trying to decide if he was worthy to be allowed into my world. I had let my guard down to let my husband in and he had fucked me over and had broken my heart into a million pieces. People always said that time would heal all wounds, but I didn't feel that this pain would ever go away. I believed this pain was going to stick with me until the day I died.

Cordan cleared his throat which brought me back to our conversation.

"I've noticed you haven't been acting like yourself. I just want you to know that I'm here if you ever need to talk."

Cordan was just about to get up but for some strange reason I didn't want him to go. There was definitely an attraction there for Cordan but I always was strong enough to fight the temptation. But today, something was different about his presence. Here he was in the break room trying to comfort me on his lunch break. He could have been doing something else meaningful with his hour, but he was here trying to find out why I was crying. It was then that I knew deep down, Cordan looked at me as more then just a bitch he could fuck. Maybe he actually cared for me as an individual. Today, for the first time, his presence brought me a little comfort. Just knowing that someone cared and wanted to help in my situation brought a little light to my dark mood.

"I know you probably don't want to be bothered but just know you aren't alone."

He was just about to walk away when I stopped him.

"Do you remember when you first asked me to lunch and you told me that you had been married before?"

"Yeah, I remember that day," he admitted.

"I'm curious to know, why did you and your wife divorce?"

Cordan's mood instantly changed. He took a seat but I could tell by his rigid demeanor that the question brought him pain.

"If you don't want to talk about it, I understand," I stated emotionally.

"No, I think it's time that I finally told my story. You will be the first one who I've opened up to," he admitted.

Cordan cleared his throat before beginning.

"I was deeply in love with my wife. I thought she could do no wrong. I put her on this pedestal only to find out that she was far from an angel. One day, I just happen to get off work early because I wasn't feeling well. I went home to find her in our bed with our neighbor. I lost it right then and there, and nearly killed both of them. The only thing that stopped me from shooting them was my career. I had worked so hard to get to my position, and I didn't want to lose it by killing them and going to prison. If I wouldn't have had this career or anything to lose, I would have gladly served my time in prison for killing them. I was so distraught over the entire thing that I couldn't even get out of bed to go to work. I was in a bad place in my life back then. A few days later after me walking in on her with our neighbor, she filed for divorce and left me. Luckily we didn't have any kids. I haven't seen her in over two years and I hope I never see her again."

"How did you get over what she had done to you?" I asked gently.

Cordan sighed.

"I still haven't gotten over her betrayal. I take it one day at a time, and with time I do believe that one day when I think of her I won't feel this pain in my chest."

"I understand."

I wiped the last bit of tears from my wet cheeks before looking into his pretty brown eyes. When I peered into them, I saw the hurt and the pain behind them, so I knew that if anyone could understand, it was him. I took a deep breath as I came to the decision to open up to him.

"I just found out recently that my husband has been cheating on me. I can honestly say that with time I could get over him cheating and still will be able to continue with my marriage, but in my situation, it's complicated. I believe he actually has feelings for this other bitch; he may even love her. Right now, he is all over the place. He's telling me he doesn't want to lose his family, but he isn't taking any action in cutting this other bitch off. Just last night, he took me to dinner to talk about our marriage only for it to be interrupted by her calling him. I'm just so angry right now. I've always been faithful to my husband and for him to betray me and be so cold about it, is what's killing me. We have two kids together and I hate the thought of being a single mother. I'm pregnant with my third child and I'm just so emotionally stressed."

"I first want to say congrats on your baby, and secondly, that you need to try to calm down and try to focus on having a healthy pregnancy."

"I'm not concerned with my pregnancy, my baby is doing fine, its just I want my marriage to work."

"Okay, that's understandable, but you need to ask yourself does your husband want that as well?"

"He says he does."

"Okay, then ask yourself is he doing what it takes to get your marriage where it used to be before this other chick came along."

I became quiet.

"It's like he has intentions, but its like he is torn between me and her. There shouldn't be any competition. I'm the mother of his kids, we have history together. We have been married since we were eighteen. There is nothing that little bitch can have on me."

Cordan nodded his head but remained quiet as I continued to compare what I had with my husband to what he didn't have with this other chick.

"Alonna, if I were you, I wouldn't press the issue. I would fall all the way back. I know you may not want to hear this but this is the best decision you can do. People tend to take advantage of someone that they have never been without. He's used to you always being there through the good times and the bad. Sometimes men, me included, take our women for granted. Not intentionally, but it does happen. He already knows what he has with you, but right now it seems he is fixated on this other woman for whatever reason. She is something different; a breath of fresh air. She is probably exciting to him for whatever reason. He can't give you a straight answer about working things out if he doesn't know himself. Logically, he may know staying with is wife and kids is the best option for him, but maybe he isn't thinking logically right now. Give him time to find out what he wants."

As Cordan continued to talk, I knew deep down he had told me everything that I had been thinking in my mind but was to scared to believe.

"Look at this as a test Alonna, just to see how strong your marriage is. If you and him can both get past this difficult time, then you will know that you and him are still meant to be together."

"And what will happen if we don't get past this? What happens if he realizes that I'm not the one he loves?"

"Then you will pick yourself up and raise your kids.

You're a beautiful strong black woman; you are going to get through this, and I'm here if you ever need me."

"Thanks Cordan for spending your entire lunch break talking to me."

"Anytime," Cordan replied before standing up to leave.

He was halfway to the door when he turned around and looked back at me. His eyes locked with mine and I felt the butterflies dancing in my stomach.

"I'm not trying to be thirsty or nothing, but I was wondering if you were interested in exchanging numbers, just in case you may want to talk outside of work hours?"

If this man would have asked me this a few weeks prior I would have cursed him out and gave him the cold shoulder, but after finally sitting down and hearing his story and being able to finally express myself to him, I instantly felt a connection. I didn't think twice about pulling out my phone and exchanging numbers with him. At this point in time, I felt he was the only real friend who understood what I was going through. With him by my side, I felt that I could get through anything.

DREW

I have never been the type of nigga who gets depressed about shit, but since Desiree had been comatose, I was feeling like I was losing my mind. I hated to get up in the morning, and I was beginning to lose money because I wasn't pushing my product as hard as I was before. Might as well say a nigga was down on his luck and I didnt see anything turning around anytime soon. I had been coming to the hospital nearly everyday to see my baby, Desiree, and still, there haven't been any changes. I had spoken to her doctor numerous times and there wasn't anything that he could tell me but to be patient with the process.

Patience was something I didn't have.

Her family was taking Desiree's comatose state just as hard as I was. Her parents and sister came nearly every day and we had finally come to a mutual understanding. Desiree's mother Debbie wasn't as cold as she was when she first met me. Things were slowly changing and her family was beginning to see me as the man that their daughter was in love with before the accident.

I had just gotten a new supply of drugs in and had just left my brother Tip's club when I decided to head to the hospital so I could sit with Desiree for a while. I pulled up at the hospital thirty minutes later and headed to her room. Luckily, I was able to sit with her and not have her family present. I slowly walked over to Desiree's bed and leaned down to place a kiss on her cheek. I rubbed my fingers through her hair just before taking a seat by her bed side. I held her hand as I spoke to her softly.

"Baby, you just don't know how much I miss you. If you can hear me, please wake up and come home. I can barely function without you. You're all I can think about. I wake up with you on my mind and I go to bed every night wishing I could hold you in my arms. Just when we were about to have our happily ever after this happens."

The beeping of the machine echoed in the quiet room. I lowered my head and kissed the top of her hand. I sat there for nearly two hours and continued to express just how much I missed her and how my life was going since she wasn't here with me. Before leaving I made sure to kiss her on her forehead before telling her that I loved her. I walked out of the hospital with tears in my eyes.

A nigga was in pain and I didn't know what I was going to do to get myself right again. I was just about to hop in my car when my phone started ringing. I picked up when I saw that it was Red calling me.

"What up partna?"

"Shit, just leaving the hospital. I came up here to visit Desiree."

"How she doing?"

"Ain't shit changed bruh, I'm beginning to lose my fucking mind."

"I know you are, but you are going to get through this. I

hate seeing you fucked up. Look, why don't you come over later tonight? I'm having a small get together at the house."

"Nah, I'm straight bruh. I don't feel like being around people."

Red sighed.

"I know you don't want to be around nobody, but you need to get out a little bit. Just come over, we can roll up and have a few beers."

"I'mma think on it."

"Yeah, do that Drew."

I ended the call with Red and headed straight to the house. My stomach started grumbling, but I wasn't in the mood to cook anything. I ended up fixing a ham and a turkey sandwich instead. I chewed my food down and swallowed, even though eating was the last thing I wanted to do. After eating half of my sandwich, I ended up throwing the rest away and heading to my bedroom where I fell across the bed and into a deep sleep.

I woke up a few hours later and rubbed the sleep from my eyes. I checked my phone and noticed that Red had hit me up a few times. I groaned as I shot him a message that I wasn't going to come over, that I was going to stay my black ass home. I was just about to lay back down across the bed when my phone started ringing.

As soon as I picked up I heard trap music in the background.

"Drew stop fucking around, get your ass over here and have a few drinks with me," Red slurred into the phone.

"Nah, I'm good bruh, I'm just going to stay home and chill."

"Lame," Red joked.

"You staying home isn't going to change anything, you're letting your life pass you by. Desiree wouldn't want that shit," Red added.

I sighed.

Even though Red was drunk as fuck, he spoke the truth. There was no way Desiree would approve of my behavior.

"Give me another hour and I will be pulling up."

"That's my boy, see you soon!" Red shouted into the phone before hanging up.

I got up, stretched, and headed to the bathroom to shower and brush my teeth. I stared at myself in the bathroom mirror and groaned. I looked a mess. My hair needed to be cut and my beard needed to be trimmed. I hadn't fixed myself up since Desiree had her accident. I had let myself go. Now I understood what Red and my brother Tip was trying to tell me. I had slipped into a deep depression and it was time that I found a way to get out this dark place.

After taking care of my hygiene, I looked inside my closet to find something to wear. I grabbed a pair of my favorite burgundy cargo shorts, a black and burgundy shirt, and a pair of black Jordan's. I grabbed my Atlanta cap and placed it on top of my head. I put on my diamond cut earrings and applied a little cologne. When I was done getting dressed, I headed out the door towards my Grey Camaro and hopped inside.

Red didn't stay far from where I lived and the traffic wasn't too thick either. I arrived at Red's crib in fifteen minutes and parked on the side of the road because there wasn't anywhere else to park. His yard was just that crowded with cars.

This was far from a little get together like he had claimed over the phone. I locked my car up and headed into Red's crib. As soon as I stepped inside, I was met with weed smoke. Music was blasting and bitches were drinking and popping their asses on niggas. I spotted Red on the living room couch snorting a line of coke with some female that I had never seen before.

"Red," I yelled out over the music.

"Drew, you finally got your ass over here!" Red yelled out as he stood up and headed over to where I was standing. He dapped me up and told me to follow him to the kitchen. He pulled out two beers and handed me one.

"Red, you told me it was going to be something small."

Red chuckled.

"Well, it started small but shit it got deep as fuck about an hour ago. Where your girl at anyway?"

I had met his ole lady a few times and I knew right off jump that she wasn't the type of bitch who liked people in her house. Shit, I was barely allowed over here my damn self and me and Red were homies.

"Shit, my little bitch gone for the weekend. She at some type of work shit out of town. By the time she gets back, everyone will be gone and she ain't gonna ever know."

I shook my head as I sipped on my beer.

"Dude, you need to fucking relax. Come on, follow me. I got some good shit that we can smoke on."

Smoking a blunt seemed like the best thing for me to do so I could try to calm myself down. It wasn't a point in me stressing about shit that I couldn't change. Desiree's situation was out of my hands and it was time that I realized the shit no matter how hard it hurt.

I followed Red back into the living room and took a seat by the chick he had just snorted a line of coke with. She was caramel in complexion with dark brown eyes. Her weave was down her back and her nails were freshly done. She was dressed in a see through white tank top with a pair of black booty shorts. She was fine, but she wasn't my type.

I saw her checking me out but I ignored her. I wasn't here to get no bitch, I only came because Red wanted to cheer me up and get my mind off Desiree.

"Damn, you fine!" the mystery girl yelled over the music.

Red was busy rolling the blunt but I know he heard what she had just said.

"If you looking for a dick to ride on I ain't the one to fuck with."

The girl rolled her eyes and crossed her chest.

"So you got a bitch already?"

"Yes, I do. Your services will not be needed."

The girl got up from beside me and told Red she was leaving.

Red didn't respond to her statement, instead he lit our first blunt and took a puff.

The mystery girl rolled her eyes and stomped off.

"Who the fuck was she?"

"Shit, I don't know, she came with one of my neighbors. I don't even know her name," Red admitted.

I shook my head and took the blunt from him and inhaled the smoke into my lungs.

I leaned my head back on the couch as Red and I passed the blunt back and forth. Half way through the joint, for the first time, I started feeling at peace. It was like nothing around me mattered.

I watched as Red snorted another line of coke. He wiped his nose and cut two more lines before asking me if I wanted to hit. I put the rest of the blunt out that I was smoking on and hit two lines back to back.

"Fuck!" I yelled.

Red laughed.

"I told your ass I had some good shit for you."

I hardly snorted coke, but tonight was an exception. I was going through a lot of shit. I needed to get high. Red and I snorted a few more lines and after that a nigga was done for the night. I was feeling real good and didn't have a care in the world.

"I'm about to head to the bathroom, I will be right back."

"Cool," Red replied.

I took the last sip of my beer before putting it down and heading to the back to the bathroom. I was so fucking high that I could barely feel my damn legs. I stepped into the bathroom, closed the door behind me, and took a long piss, before shaking my dick and washing my hands.

I was heading out the bathroom when I spotted a nigga penning some chick up against the wall, and was trying to force himself on her.

I mean damn, everyone in this party was getting high and drunk, but this nigga couldn't have been too high that he was trying to rape a bitch in front of a crowd of people. It angered me that people were just standing around drinking and dancing and no one seemed to notice this girl crying out for help. I didn't know who the female was, but I wasn't about to let this nigga rape her.

I walked over to the dude who was now sticking his tongue down the chick's mouth as he tried to tear off her panties with is other hand.

I didn't think twice when I pushed him off the chick who was crying for him to stop.

"Nigga, who the fuck you think you is?" he asked me furiously.

"You need to leave that chick alone, she doesn't want you touching on her dog. Are you really trying to rape shorty in front of all these people?"

"Who the fuck do you think you is? That bitch want this dick. Stay out my fucking business," he spat at me.

He was just about to grab shorty again but I punched him in the jaw. These folks were so wasted that they continued to dance on each other even though I had just punched a nigga out.

I thought one blow would serve him right, but the lick

only angered him. He stood up on wobbly legs and charged after me.

I hit him one last time in the face and he fell to the floor. The chick was just about to get raped if I would have done nothing. She slowly walked over to where the nigga was laid out at and stomped on him a few times with her stilettoes.

"You nasty ass freak," she spat.

"Are you okay?" I asked her gently.

I could tell that she had been crying so I wanted to make sure that she was good.

"Thanks for saving me. If you wouldn't have come, I don't know what would have happened," she choked out.

I understood exactly what the chick was thinking. I could tell that she was shaken up by the ordeal so I offered for her to follow me outside just so she could get away from all the noise.

I lead her out the back door and we sat in a chair on the back deck. This was where Red normally rolled up when his girl was home, since he wasn't allowed to smoke in the house. Sitting outside under the moonlight seemed to be something romantic that a nigga would do with a girl he was kicking it with. I knew nothing about this chick. All I wanted to do was to get her from around all the noise and to make sure that she was okay. Her eyes were still filled with tears, but from what I could see, she didn't have any bruises on her. She was still shaking but she was beginning to try to calm herself down.

"Do you smoke?" I asked her.

"No, I don't," she replied quietly.

Giving her weed to calm her nerves seemed to be out of the question.

"I just want to say thanks again for what you did back there."

"You're welcome," I replied.

As the moon light shined down on us, I couldn't help but notice just how beautiful she was. She was light brown in complexion with almond shaped eyes. She looked to be about 5'2 in height, and had a nicely shaped body. Her lips were full, but not too thick, and was colored with red lipstick. Her long weave stopped at her ass. I instantly began to feel guilty once my manhood started to come to attention. The crazy thing was, my dick hadn't gotten on hard since Desiree had been in the hospital. Sex had been the last thing on my mind lately, but as I sat beside this chocolate beauty, I couldn't stop the thought from running through my head.

"Well, I'm glad you're okay. I should be going," I commented.

I had to get away from her before I ended up doing some shit that I would later regret. I now knew that nothing was wrong with me sexually, I just hadn't been tempted to fuck on anyone. Now that I was attracted to someone, it was time for me to avoid the situation at all costs.

"Oh, I'm sorry. I should have figured that you were here with someone, and here I am with you outside trying to make sure I'm okay."

I cleared my throat and stood up from my chair.

"The nigga who throwing this party is my homeboy. I came alone, I'm not here with anyone."

I didn't know if I was high as fuck or if I was just seeing things, but I should have sworn that I saw this girl eyes sparkle once I told her that information.

"I'm here alone, too. I came with my homegirl, but she ditched my ass when her crazy ass boyfriend came and dragged her out the party an hour ago."

"Damn, so you telling me you don't know anybody here?"

"Not a single soul. I was trying to a way home since I rode with her here. Neither one of us knew that her nigga had tracked her here. Honestly, I stayed behind because I didn't want to get in the middle of their argument."

"That's understandable."

Even though I was high as hell, I still knew what I was doing. I wasn't completely out of it to the point that I didn't know what was going on. Giving her a ride home seemed like the right thing to do, even though my mind told me to just call her an Uber. Leaving her to find her own way home when I knew she was still tipsy wouldn't have been right.

"Look if you need a ride home, I can take you. I'm about to leave anyway."

"Cool," she replied with a small smile on her face.

DREW

"*W*hat's your name, lil' mama?" I asked the girl after she had slid into my car.

"My name is Kinsley."

"Nice to meet ya, Kinsley. I'm Drew."

Kinsley clicked her seat belt in and told me the address that she wanted to be dropped off at. We rode in silence for a while before she turned towards me and tried to make conversation.

"I appreciate the ride."

"No problem, you live in the same direction that I was going to take to go home, so it's all good."

Kinsley smiled before closing her eyes.

The sweet smell of her perfume filled my nose and her presence in my car was really fucking with me. I needed to hurry and get her ass home as soon as I could. I was halfway to her spot when she popped her eyes open and started asking me personal questions about my girl. The bitch was fishing, and I was curious to know what she was trying to find out.

"How long you and girl been together?" Kinsley asked innocently.

"Why do you want to know?"

"Oh, I'm just curious. It's one in the morning, and here you are with me taking me home, when you should be home laid up under her."

I gripped the steering wheel tightly because she was right. I had no business being out this late with her in my car, but what I was doing was a good deed. I was making sure she was getting home safe, at least that was what I was telling myself.

"Do y'all live together?"

"Why do you want to know?" I asked bluntly.

"I was just wondering, that's all."

We pulled up at her spot a few moments later, but she didn't make an attempt to get out of the car.

"You know you can come in if you want to," Kinsley offered.

"No, I'm good on that lil mama."

Kinsley pouted.

Now, everything was beginning to make sense. She was asking all these damn questions because she was trying to see if she could sneak her some dick in tonight. I wanted to laugh because the shit was comical.

"I suggest you head inside. It's getting late and I need to be getting back home."

"I'm going to head inside, but first I got one last thing to do," Kinsley replied tipsily.

"What is that?" I asked her curiously.

Kinsley smirked before she leaned in towards me and placed a kiss on my lips.

When she placed her lips on mine, it was like my entire body was awaken. My dick instantly grew hard, and that's when I knew I was in trouble.

"I love me a dark chocolate nigga with a beard. I've been wanting to kiss you since you saved me. I don't care if you have a girl, I'm drunk as fuck and I want some dick," Kinsley whispered in my ear bluntly.

"*Fuck!*" I screamed in my head.

I wanted some pussy so badly but the thought of fucking another bitch besides Desiree wasn't something I needed to be doing. Desiree had my heart, but this fine ass chick right here was begging for me to break her back in. A part of me told me to push that bitch out my car, while the other part told me to give her exactly what she wanted. I was so deep in thought on if I should fuck her or not that Kinsley had took it upon herself to make a go of it while I was distracted.

She had already unzipped my pants and was on the verge of pulling my dick out when I pushed her hand away.

"Damn, what the fuck you doing?"

Kinsley chuckled.

"I'm about to make the decision for you. I'm about to take your ass to heaven," she replied seductively.

I wanted to stop her but as soon as she took my manhood into her wet mouth, I knew that I had lost the battle. I closed my eyes as she made love to my magic stick with her mouth.

"Shit," I moaned as she twirled her tongue around my mushroom head.

I pushed her head further down on my love stick until she started choking.

"You wanted to suck some dick, well suck that shit right," I said to her as I pushed her head in an up and down motion.

She was sucking my dick so damn good that the bitch had my toes curling. If her head was this good, I was beginning to wonder how the pussy was. I didn't have to wait long to find out though. She pulled her mouth off my pole and immediately lifted her dress up to her stomach and pulled her panties to the side.

"I'm tired of sucking dick, I want to see what that dick like."

As soon as she sat down on my pole, I knew that I wasn't going to be able to last long. Her pussy was super wet and tight like a glove. Her cries filled my ears as she rocked back and forth on my magic stick. She was grinding her honey box on my tool so hard, that the car was shaking. I pulled her dress from over her titties and sucked on each of her nipples as she rode my stick.

"I'm about to cum," she cried out in my ear.

I busted first and she followed right behind me. When we were done, she slid off of me and hurried to fix her clothes. I slid my wood back into my boxers and zipped my cargo shorts back up. I rolled the windows down so we could get some air, and watched her as she lit up a cigarette.

"I thought you ain't smoke?"

"You asked if I smoked weed. I smoke cigarettes."

When she grabbed her phone from her purse, I wasn't expecting her to boldly ask for my number.

"I really think we need to keep in touch," she stated.

I have never been the type of nigga to become speechless after getting some pussy, but this chick had really fucked me to the point that I could barely catch my breath. She had fucked me so good that I couldn't even respond right off.

"I guess you don't want me to have your number. Cool," Kinsely retorted once I didn't answer her question fast enough.

I finally snapped out of the trance that I was in and decided to exchange numbers with her. If she got stupid, I could always block her ass, I reassured myself.

"I guess I'm going to head inside. I hope to hear from you soon," Kinsley stated.

Just before she stepped out my car, she leaned in and slid

her tongue into my mouth. I instantly responded by kissing her back. She pulled away a few moments later and stepped out my car. I waited until she had made it into her apartment before I pulled off.

As soon as she was out of my presence, that's when it all hit me. If this would have been a test on how loyal I truly was to Desiree, then I had just failed it horribly. In my moment of weakness, I had found comfort with another chick who I didn't even know. The only thing I knew about her ,was her name. I couldn't even blame it on cocaine or alcohol. It was all me. I had made the choice and it was a dumb move on my part, and the scary shit about it was, I ain't even think to wrap my dick up.

Everything happened so damn fast. The only thing I could do was hope that none of this come back to haunt me.

ALONNA

*J*awan's calls continued to go unanswered. I didn't have shit to say to him, and there was no forgiving him, either. I was doing exactly what Cordan had suggested. I was leaving him alone so he could figure out who, and what he wanted. I wasn't about to run behind no nigga; not even my husband.

The dinging of my phone told me that I had a text message. I figured it was another text from Jawan, but wasn't expecting it to be from Cordan. I opened it immediately just to see what he wanted.

Cordan: I'm just checking on you to make sure you're okay.

I smiled as I reread the message a few times before finally responding.

Alonna: I'm okay. I'm doing what you told me to do, I'm giving him space.

Cordan: Has he reached out to you?

Alonna: Yes, he has been blowing up my phone for three days, but I never respond.

Cordan: Smh, eventually he gonna pull up.

Alonna: Tough luck, because I ain't going to answer the door.

Cordan: Lol. Okay. Well I was just checking on you that's all.

Alonna: Thanks, but I'm good over this way.

I was just about to doze off when my phone dinged again.

Cordan: Would you like to come over for dinner tomorrow after work?

I laid there in bed and stared at my phone for the longest time. I didn't know how to respond to the message. There wasn't anything wrong with having dinner with him, I told myself. I had to get Jawan out of my mind and Cordan seemed like the perfect man to help me with that issue. I needed to get out and get my mind off of things, I told myself.

Alonna: Dinner sounds lovely.

I fell asleep shortly after sending that message.

I woke up the next morning well rested and ready to start my day. I told myself that it had nothing to do with the dinner invite that Cordan had offered after work, but deep down I knew it had everything to do with that. I took my time getting dressed that morning. Normally, I brushed my hair down and kept it moving, but today, I decided to wear some silver earrings and a silver necklace with my hot pink scrubs. I grabbed my black and hot pink Jordan's out of the closet and decided to put them on. I applied some lipstick to my lips and even put on some fake lashes. I was looking and smelling good heading to work. I headed out the door and hopped in my car.

After pulling up at my job, I headed inside to clock in. For the first time in a long time, I finally decided to speak and try to interact with my coworkers. Whether anyone knew it or not, Cordan had really brighten my outlook on the Jawan situation. It was time for me to get my life back. My life was not about to stop just because Jawan didn't know if he wanted to still be my husband or not.

I worked my ass off the entire day all the way up until it was time for my lunch break. My phone vibrated in my pocket letting me know I had a text.

Cordan: Are you coming to the cafeteria for lunch today?

Alonna: Yes.

Cordan: okay cool.

After doing the last bit of my rounds, I headed to the cafeteria and grabbed a turkey sandwich, chips and a Sprite. I found Cordan sitting down at a table and he was already digging into his food.

I chuckled as I took a seat in front of him.

"Looks like someone has worked up an appetite," I joked.

"You have no idea," he laughed.

We laughed and talked through our entire lunch. It felt real good to laugh again. I had been so depressed and angry lately that I never thought I would ever get back to my old self. I had a long way to go, that's for sure, but I was slowly getting myself back on track.

After we were done with our lunch, Cordan grabbed our trash and threw it away. As we headed out of the cafeteria and back to our work duties, he pulled me to the side.

"Don't forget about dinner after work."

"I don't plan on missing it," I whispered to him.

When he smiled down at me, his eyes shimmered and my heart skipped a beat. Damn, this man was fine as hell and the sad thing about it, there was nothing I could do about it. Acting on it was out of the question, at least right now it was, but I didn't know what the future held for either one of us.

When it was time for me to clock out later that day, best believe I was the first one out of the door. I rushed home and hopped my ass in the tub so I could soak and pamper myself.

Even though this wasn't a date or anything like that, I still wanted to look my best.

I soaked in the tub for over an hour before I finally stepped out. I wrapped myself in a towel and tiptoed into my bedroom in search of something to wear. I wanted to wear something sexy but nothing too revealing; I didn't want to give him the wrong idea. I was in the middle of debating to wear a mini sundress or either some blue jean shorts when my phone dinged letting me know I had a text message. I checked my messages and noticed it was the doctor's office letting me know that I had another appointment to attend early next week. I sent a confirmation email letting them know that I would definitely be present. After taking care of that, I went back to deciding what I was going to wear. I eventually ended up choosing the mini white sundress with a pair of black sandals. I put on a pair of silver hooped earrings and painted my lips with soft pink lipstick. I sprayed some perfume and slicked my hair down. Just before I left, I checked myself out in the mirror and knew that I was going to have Cordan's eyes on me all night.

Did I really want all that attention from a man who I knew was attracted to me? The best feeling in the world was being wanted and Cordan was making me feel like a woman again. I knew I was far from ugly, but now that Jawan was sprung over some other bitch, it really fucked up my ego.

I grabbed the phone off of the bed and texted Cordan to let him know that I was dressed and ready to head over to his house.

A few moments later, Cordan sent me over his address which I plugged into my GPS. I grabbed my purse and keys and headed out the door towards my car.

I blasted Cardi B and rapped along to some of her music the entire ride. I was vibing real good and was in an even better mood. There was nothing that could bring me down at this point in time, not even my husband.

I pulled up at Cordan's house thirty minutes later. It was very nice looking from the outside and he lived in a white folks housing complex where all of the houses had garages. I already knew that he was paying good ass money to live in the white folks section.

I hopped out of my car and was just about to knock on the door when the door swung open.

"Wow, you look so fucking beautiful," Cordan complimented me.

I couldn't help but blush as I stepped inside his home.

"You look good yourself," I said to him after stepping inside his crib.

He was dressed in a pair of khaki shorts with an orange polo shirt and a pair of Adidas.

Cordan smiled at me before closing the door behind me.

"Damn, you have a nice home."

"Thank you. It's a two bedroom with one and a half bathroom."

"It looks so big though to just be a two bedroom."

"Yes it is very spacious, that's for sure."

I sniffed the air and my stomach instantly began to growl. The beeping of the stove let me knew that dinner was indeed done.

"Let me take this meatloaf out the oven," Cordan commented just before he hurried into the kitchen.

I walked around the living room and was impressed by how clean his house was and how good the food smelled. Damn, was this really this nigga's house or was he using all of this to try to win me over since he knew my husband and me were on bad terms? I looked at a few of his family portraits from when he was a kid and inspected his music collection while he was in the kitchen getting things situated.

"Dinner is now served!" Cordan yelled out.

I headed into the kitchen and was shocked to see a whole damn meal prepared. There was no way in hell this man had cooked all of this himself. I stood there shocked as hell, I couldn't even speak.

"Um, I can tell by how you're looking that you weren't expecting any of this."

"You're damn right I wasn't. Now what I want to know is what bitch did you bribe to come over here and cook all this for you," I joked.

Cordan laughed at my comment.

I watched him as he grabbed our plates and started fixing our food. This man had meatloaf, which was cooked to perfection, mashed potatoes, corn bread, green beans, and he even had made some chocolate rice crispy treats.

"Have a seat, Alonna."

I took a seat at the dinner table and waited for him to set my plate in front of me. He poured me a half a glass of wine, and sat the food in front of me. I stared down at my plate then up at him.

He laughed.

"You're sure you made this by yourself?" I asked quizzically.

"Um, you can check the trash if you want to. I cooked this myself."

I grabbed my silverware and dug in. The first bite was delicious and I made sure to let him know it.

"I guess you weren't expecting me to know how to cook."

"You don't really look like the type of man who would know how to cook."

He chuckled.

"It's a lot you don't know about me, that's why I invited you over, so we could get to know each other better. You were so cold to me when we first met."

"I was cold for a reason."

"Why is that?" he asked as he sipped his wine.

"Well, I thought you were one of them hoe ass niggas who was trying to fuck all the fine ass chicks at your job."

Cordan shook his head at my comment.

"I'm far from that. I don't sleep around. I might give off a lot of sexual energy to females, but I don't go around smashing everything. I do admit, I may flirt a lot, but that's as far as it goes with anyone at my workplace. I've only had my eye on one person."

I cleared my throat and he smirked.

"I don't want to make you uncomfortable, so lets change the subject."

"Sounds good to me. What I'm curious to know is how you learned how to cook like this?"

"My mama taught me how to cook when I was growing up. Back then, she was sickly so I had to grow up early. I had to become the man of the house after my father walked out on us."

"I'm sorry to hear that."

"I was her only child so I was all she had. Back then, she was in and out of the hospital so much that I felt she was living in that bitch. I practically had to raise myself," Cordan stated sadly.

"And you did a wonderful job. I know your mother would be very proud of you."

"Yeah, she would have been, but she didn't live long enough to see me become a doctor. She died from a brain tumor when I was thirteen. I ended up having to go live with my auntie until I went off to college."

"I'm so sorry," I said sadly.

Cordan smiled weakly.

"She's the reason why I decided to go to college and become a doctor."

"And now look at you; successful and one of the best doctors at the hospital."

"I wouldn't say that, but I love all of my patients. I just want to be useful and save other people's lives, since I wasn't able to save my mother's."

"I understand," I told him softly.

We continued to talk a little about his childhood but we stayed clear of the conversation of my marriage.

"How's the pregnancy going?" he asked me gently as he grabbed my empty plate.

"This pregnancy has been stressful as hell, but I'm making it the best way I can."

"That's all you can do. Are you excited about your third child?" Cordan asked curiously.

"Do you want to hear the truth or the lie that I tell myself every day?"

"I would rather hear the truth," Cordan assured me.

I cleared my throat and took the chocolate rice crispy treat he had just cut for me. I took a bite and put the sweet dessert down.

Guilt instantly began to fill my body because no one knew how I truly felt about being pregnant but Jawan, and even though I had told him, he really didn't understand the things that I felt inside on the regular.

I cleared my throat before I finally started explaining things to Cordan.

"This pregnancy was unexpected. My first two pregnancies, I was happy, healthy, and was at a good mind set, but this pregnancy has been hard on me. I don't want any more kids, but I've come to accept that I'm pregnant now and there isn't anything I can do about it. It's just, I've had so many plans for my future and now being pregnant is going to slow down this process."

"Explain it to me, talk to me," Cordan replied gently.

I took a deep breath and went into detail.

"I have always wanted to become a registered nurse. I've been working my ass off with working at the hospital, showing good worth ethic at work and taking classes online."

"You're a damn good LPN, I assure you that," Cordan complimented me.

"Yes, but I want more. I was supposed to have finished nursing school later this year and now with this pregnancy and working it's just going to be too much. I haven't even told anyone I'm pregnant at work because I know they are going to be all sympathetic when I hit the six month mark and going to tell me to take a leave of absence. Every pregnancy has been this way. I just don't want to be slowed down. I want to reach my goals and be successful. Jawan doesn't seem to understand that. He wants me to stay home and be a housewife, but I don't want that; I ain't never wanted that."

"I understand where you're coming from, but things happen. We have our plans but the universe has its own plan. You're pregnant now. There's no going back; all you can do is live with this and learn to work around it. Don't look at it as a bad thing. You are bringing a child into this world. Some women would kill to be in your position. You work every single day and give your patients your all. You still have your whole life ahead of you to become a RN. You may be slowed down, but your goals don't have to change. You should remember, it doesn't matter how long it takes for you to reach your goal, as long as you reach them. You may not get that RN position like you want to right now, but you *will* get it, and when you do, you are going to be ready for it."

Tears fell from my eyes and he wiped them away for me.

"Thanks for talking with me about this."

"Of course, your children and your family should always come first, Alonna. I love that you're career oriented, but I would love to be able to one day have my own family as well. See, we're the same but we are after two different goals as well. As far as your husband not understanding you, you may be right. We are all different people and think differently. We are not the same and are not always meant to want the same things out of life as our partners. That's what makes us unique. All you can do is have enough love for one another to get through the differences. The goal is to make your marriage stronger and to work as a team."

"You're right."

Cordan nodded his head before standing up and grabbing me a bottle of water from the fridge.

"You need to wash that wine down that you just had. I don't want the baby in their floating."

I laughed and grabbed the water bottle from him and sipped on it.

"The food was so damn good. I enjoyed."

"I'm glad that you liked it," he replied.

I stood up and started helping him load the dishwasher.

"You ain't got to do all that, I got it. I don't want you to ruin your dress."

"This dress will be fine. I can at least help you load the dishwasher since you messed up all of these dishes to impress me."

"Did it work?"

I looked up at him and smirked.

"Maybe," I chuckled.

After helping him load the dishwasher, I pulled out my phone and noticed I had over ten missed calls. All of them were from Jawan. Good thing I had put my phone on silent.

"It's getting late, I should get going."

I headed to the door with him following behind me.

"You don't have to leave right now. We don't have to work tomorrow."

He grabbed me by my arm and turned me around to face him.

I took a few steps back until my back was pressed up against his front door. Goosebumps covered my arms, and my heart skipped a beat when he softly caressed my neck with his finger.

"You're so beautiful tonight."

"Thank you," I choked out.

I wanted to run, but I couldn't seem to move either one of my feet. It was like, I was frozen in place. I held my breath as he stared down at my lips. I knew he wanted to kiss me, and deep down, I wanted him to kiss me, too.

When he leaned in I met him half way and that's when sparks began to fly as our lips touched. I slid my tongue into his mouth and we kissed each other passionately. He closed the distance between us and wrapped his arm my waist as he deepened our kiss. When the kiss ended, my brain felt fuzzy.

"You taste so fucking good."

I slowly opened my eyes and noticed he was still staring down at me. It was just a kiss, but it felt like so much more. He caressed my cheek with his thumb before he explored my mouth yet again. I dropped my purse on the floor as he picked me up with one arm.

Cordan carried me towards his brown leather couch and laid me down. When he started kissing and sucking on my neck, my pussy instantly got to dripping.

I moaned softly as he pulled my dress down and started sucking on each of my erect nipples.

"Yessss," I cried out.

"I want you so damn bad. I've been wanting you for a long time. Tonight is about pleasing you. I want to make you cum, " Cordan stated.

I pulled him to me and slid my tongue into his mouth as I wrapped my legs around his waist.

"I want you, too," I moaned into his ear.

He pulled away from me a few moments later and slid my dress up over my stomach and slid my thong to the side. He dipped a finger into my honey pot and I instantly lost all control of myself.

"Cordan," I moaned as he slid another finger into my wetness.

He played in my love nest as he sucked on my neck. I closed my eyes tightly and cried out his name. After sucking on my neck he started placing kisses on my face and then slid his tongue into my mouth. When the kiss was broken, he immediately fell to his knees and started sucking on my pussy.

I whimpered as he licked and sucked on my clit. It wasn't long before I started cumming. My legs started to shake, and my body grew weak as he licked my pussy juices clean. When he was done, we shared a deep and passionate kiss. My body was so weak that I couldn't even move. Cordan pulled my dress back into place just before he took a seat beside me. We were both quiet and I guess we both were in our thoughts. This was the first time that I had ever cheated on Jawan. Did I feel guilty? No, not really. I'm sure at this very moment he was somewhere blowing Monay's back out. I wasn't about to ruin the best head that I had just gotten thinking about my ex. If Cordan's head was this damn good and could make me cum with no dick involved, then I knew his dick game was on point. Maybe, just maybe, if we both played our cards right, I was going to get a sample of that dick one of these days.

As I laid on his chest, I only prayed that what Cordan and I had just done wouldn't cause any issues later on in the future. I only hoped that I hadn't made a mistake, but as Cordan rubbed his hand gently over my arm, I knew that what had just happened had been something beautiful.

MONAY

Two Days Later...

"Mama, you really need to eat," I fussed as I stood over the stove to finish cooking grits, eggs, and bacon.

"I'm not hungry, Monay. I feel sick to my damn stomach. I can't eat that shit."

I sighed and cut the stove off in frustration.

"What about soup? You want me to make some soup instead?"

"Uggh, you know I hate soup. I didn't eat the shit while I was in good health, I damn sure ain't going to eat it now."

I shook my head and walked over to where she was sitting in the kitchen chair.

"Mama, you haven't eaten anything today. It's late in the afternoon. It's time to put something on your stomach. Look, I'm about to let you roll some weed. Maybe that will give you an appetite."

"I'm good, I don't want to smoke," she fussed.

"Okay fine. I'm going to run to the store and get you some

Ensure. It will at least give you some nutrition since you don't want to eat your food."

Mama didn't say anything. She only stared into space. I was near tears as I kissed her on the cheek and told her that I was going to let her sit in the living room until I got back.

I was just about to help her out of her seat, when she told me sternly she didn't need my help. I didn't leave her side until she made her way into the living room and was comfortable. I flicked on the TV and turned it to the Lifetime channel.

"Okay Mama, I'm going up the road to the store. I will be right back."

Again, Mama didn't speak. She continued to stare at the TV screen. I grabbed my purse, keys, and made sure to lock the door behind me. I was just about to head to the store when Jawan pulled up. My heart skipped a beat when he got out. He was looking sexy as hell in his white and black Nike shirt, with a pair of black cargo shorts, and some black Nikes.

"Where are you running off to?" He asked as he walked over to my car.

"I'm trying to go to the grocery store to get my mama some Ensure. She ain't eating. I can't get her to eat anything anymore, and it's frustrating as hell."

"I know it is, but I can go get it for you. Stay home with your mama."

I looked up at him and saw sympathy in his eyes.

"You don't have to do all of that," I told him urgently.

"I promised you that I was always going to be here for you and I meant that shit. If you need anything, all you gotta do is let me know, and I got you baby."

Hearing him saying that shit really brought joy to my heart, but as soon as my heart began to swell with love, everything changed when I thought about his situation with his wife. Had anything changed since he said that he was planning on us being together?

I wanted to ask him but I knew it wasn't the time. I had other pressing matters that needed to be attended to. I guess Jawan must have read my mind because he quickly told me that when he got back, we could talk. I nodded my head in agreement and headed back into the house with my mama.

"Well Mama, Jawan just stopped by. He's going to go to the store to get you something."

"I don't know why you trying to force me to eat when I ain't hungry."

I knew fussing with my mama was a losing battle, so I ignored her comment.

"While we wait, I'm going to comb your hair for you."

I headed to my bedroom and grabbed a comb and some grease and headed back to where she was sitting on the couch. I combed through her fine hair, greased her scalp, and braided her hair into two braids.

"There you go, all done."

"Thanks Monay," Mama said before ushering for me to sit next to her.

"I assume you and Jawan have made up?"

"No, not really. But we are going to get a chance to talk things out when he gets back."

"Good, because I really like him," Mama stated.

"I like him, too."

An hour later, Jawan was knocking at the front door. I let him in and grabbed the bag that he held in his hand.

"Hey Mama Gwen. How are you feeling?" Jawan asked her before embracing her in a hug.

"I'm making it. I wish this child of mine would stop treating me like a newborn baby."

Jawan chuckled.

"I'm sure it's all out of love."

"Yeah, I know it is. She has gone over and beyond to make sure I'm okay."

"That's what daughters do," I commented.

"Not when they had a shitty mother."

The room grew quiet.

"Mama that's the past. Let us focus on the present and our future."

I took the nutritional shakes from out of the grocery bag and opend one of the bottles. I passed it to Mama and told her that she better drink all of it if she didn't want to eat any food. She sniffed the bottle before turning her head.

I folded my arms over my chest and told her I didn't want to hear any complaints.

Mama groaned, but drank the bottle of the nutritional shake as she was told.

"Okay Jawan, while Mama is enjoying her breakfast, lunch, and dinner, we can talk."

"Okay cool," he replied.

I was just about to head outside when he grabbed me.

"We gonna talk about this outside?"

"Yeah, why not?"

Jawan stared from me to my mama, but sighed.

"Okay cool. Outside will be fine."

I closed the door behind us and took a seat in one of the chairs that was on our porch.

"For once in your life, I want you to be real with me."

Jawan cleared his throat, "I will tell you everything that you want to know."

"No, I want you to tell me the truth, no matter what you think I want to hear. Don't hold nothing back from me."

"Okay," Jawan replied.

I took a deep breath and asked my first question.

"Do you really love me, or was it all fun and games for you?"

Jawan grabbed me by my hand and told me to look at him.

"Baby, I do love you. I never thought that I could love another woman other than my wife, but after meeting you that day when your car broke down, and after getting to spend time with you, I couldn't get enough of you no matter how hard I tried to pull away. I've never cheated on my wife, never met anyone who I would want to risk my family to be with, until I met you. The crazy thing is, we haven't even had sex. That's how I know what we have is real."

I listened and stared into his eyes just to see if I saw any deception there, but so far, I felt like he was telling the truth.

"Next question. Are you really going to leave your pregnant wife for me?"

Jawan became silent. I stared over at him and noticed that he was in deep thought. Just when he was finally about to answer, I raised my hand to silence.

"Answer this question truthfully because if you lie to me, I swear you will lose me forever."

"I love my wife Monay. I'm not going to lie about that, she is always going to have a part of my heart because she is the mother of my kids, and we have been married since teenagers. At one point in time, she was the only woman I wanted to spend the rest of my life with, until I met you. I'm not going to lie, I'm going to keep it real with you. I want to keep my wife and my family, but I also want to keep you, as well. I don't want to let go of either one of you. I love both of ya'll, I truly do."

I felt like someone had stabbed me in the heart. Deep down, I should have known that he wasn't going to leave his wife for me. She was pregnant by him with their third child. What sort of man would he be to abandon his entire family for me? That would only put him in the same type of category that I had placed my father into when he left me and

Mama, and never wanted to be in my life. The shit was painful for a child. I, of all people, knew the pain that the kids would endure, but still. Where in the hell did that leave me?

Instead of appearing weak and crying after hearing the truth, I knew that I had to suck it up and dig deeper.

"Where is this relationship going? Are you really trying to keep me as some side chick?"

"Monay you are not a side chick, I don't look at you as one and you shouldn't look at yourself as one."

I rolled my eyes.

"But that's what I thought. That's what you call someone who isn't your man squeeze."

Jawan grew quiet.

"I don't want to let you go, Monay. I can't let you go."

I sat there for the longest time, deep in my thoughts. Would I accept the role of being his side bitch, or would I cut him out my life for good? I wanted to be with this man, I did, but was it even worth it if I wasn't going to be his number one?

Jawan must have known that I was thinking on the matter because he reached over, and caressed my hand.

"I don't want to pressure you into doing something you don't want to do, but at this time this is all I can offer you. I know it's fucked up, but I can't abandon my kids, not right now. My wife is stressing the issue of cutting things off with you. She's bitter and angry that I haven't blocked you, but I can't do that because you have a place in my heart, too. My wife is going to be pissed for a very long time for me falling in love with someone else, but eventually, we all will get over this and be able to move on with our lives."

"You mean you and your wife will eventually be able to work through you betraying her and moving on with your lives? Remember, you just basically told me that you're not committed to me."

I stood up to walk into the house but Jawan stopped me.

"Baby, I love you, I know you don't want to hear this shit right now, but I mean it. If I didn't want to be with you, I would have fucked you that day in my condo and you would have never heard from me again. What we have is special."

"Yeah, its special, but apparently it isn't strong enough to break up a marriage now, is it?"

Jawan stared down at me and I saw the pain and heartache in his eyes. I was asking him to make a tough decision. Was I being too selfish, or was I acting like any typical female would when they were in love? I was tired of niggas pushing me aside to give their hearts to bitches they felt deservered it. What about Me? Didn't I deserve to be happy? Didn't I deserve to have a man who was going to love and cherish me? I asked myself.

I had to get my ass in the house and away from him so I could think. Jawan was standing only inches apart from me. I held my breath as he leaned in and placed a kiss on my lips. At first I stood frozen not wanting to open myself up to him ever again, but when he caressed my cheek with his finger and whispered that he was going to be in my life forever, I fell deep into my feelings and there was no going back.

Jawan was my addiction and I needed my fix. As our lips caressed for the second time, I opened my mouth up towards him and our tongues danced together. He held me gently up against him as we explored one another. The kiss was passionate, sweet, and demanding. When the kiss finally ended, I still clung to his shirt and was too scared to let him go.

"Promise me that you will always remain loyal and faithful to me," Jawan demanded.

I stared up at Jawan and was mesmerized by what I saw in

his eyes. "I promise," I replied softly before he placed a kiss on each of my fingers.

"I promise that I will always love and cherish you."

I was in love with this man. I only hoped that my heart wouldn't end up broken in the end.

ALONNA

For this entire weekend you might as well say that I had been spending it with Cordan and I had been enjoying myself to the fullest. When I was around Cordan, I didn't think of Jawan or what he may be doing since he wasn't living with me. He had been calling me all weekend, but I had been ignoring him because there wasn't shit that we had to talk about.

I thought that after Cordan had eaten my pussy that he was going to start acting all crazy and shit, but he was the complete opposite. He hadn't pushed the issue about sex, and I didn't feel awkward around him. The only thing I felt was happiness and peacefulness when we were around each other. He was the perfect gentleman. He had spoiled me this weekend with his cooking. I honestly enjoyed watching TV, talking and playing board games with him. Even though I went home every night to my own house, I still would lie in bed and think about him until I would fall asleep.

Jawan hadn't crossed my mind any this weekend and that's how I knew I was doing the right thing. It wasn't healthy for me to be wrapped up in what my husband was doing. If he wasn't talking about cutting Monay off and being a family, then I didn't want to hear shit that he had to say. I refused to let his indecisiveness and stupidity keep me depressed and down.

After leaving Cordan's house Sunday night, I headed straight home to find Jawan parked in the driveway. He was the last person I wanted to see. I stepped out of my car and Jawan got out of his.

"Where have you been? I've been blowing your line up."

"I don't know what for. You've been blowing up the wrong bitch. You need to be checking for that other bitch."

"Alonna, baby please, let's talk. I love my family."

"I don't give a fuck about any of that shit. I don't want to hear anything you have to say because you ain't gotten rid of that other bitch. Matter of fact, does the little bitch even know you're over here trying to persuade me to talk to you? Are you seriously trying to figure out which one of us you can make into a side bitch of yours? Well let me tell you something, nigga. I will never downgrade from wife to some side bitch. If I don't come first, then I don't want to have shit to do with you."

Jawan grabbed me and told me to give him time to explain.

"Nigga, you can't tell me shit because you don't even know who or what you want. That young bitch has gotten to you. You ain't using your fucking brain. Apparently you're thinking with your dick. You want your family, huh? That's what you're telling me, right?"

"Yes, Alonna, we just need to talk. I'm sure we can work this out."

I laughed at him.

"Have you left Monay yet? Have you cut that bitch off? Have you blocked her number?"

Jawan stood there looking stupid as hell. I shook my head and pulled away from him.

"Like I thought, get the fuck out my face, bruh," I spat at him before walking into the house and slamming it behind me.

I stood there with my body pressed up against the door until I heard him pull off. I sighed with relief that he had left. My heart was aching, but eventually I was going to get over the shit. I headed into my bathroom and removed my clothes before cutting on the shower. When the water was hot enough, I stepped inside and washed the scent of Cordan off of me. I closed my eyes as the hot water hit my face, the only person I thought about was Cordan and how his mouth felt over my body. I washed myself clean and stepped out of the shower thirty minutes later.

I headed into my bedroom to find some bed clothes to wear. After getting dressed in a pair of white booty shorts, red tube top, and a pair of red socks, I slid under my covers and grabbed my phone off the nightstand when I heard a ding. I opened it to see that I had text from Cordan. I smiled when I noticed that it was a message asking if I had made it home safely.

I replied back to let him know that I had made it home and that I had just gotten out of the shower and was heading to bed. It was damn near one in the morning, and I was tired as hell. Cordan sent me a bunch of kissy faces before telling me to have a good night. I went to bed with a big smile on my face.

* * *

I WOKE up at three in the morning in pain. The pain was so terrible that I was barely even able to move. I pulled the covers off of my body and turned on my night stand light. That's when I noticed I was bleeding. I tried to get off the bed to go to the bathroom, but fell back down on the bed screaming in pain. I knew all too well, that something was definitely wrong.

Tears fell from my eyes as I reached for my phone. I needed a way to the hospital and I needed to go ASAP. The person I decided to call was my husband. Even though I was angry at him, I knew he would want to know if something was wrong with the baby.

I called Jawan over five times, but he never picked up the phone. I cried out again as a sharp pain tore through my uterus. I went to my messages and sent him a text to let him know I needed him to take me to the emergency room because I was in pain and bleeding. After not getting a response back, I decided the only person I could call was Cordan. I hated to wake him but I had to get to the hospital and Jawan hadn't reached out to me.

Cordan picked up on the second ring and asked if I was okay.

"Please come get me and take me to the emergency room if you can. I'm in pain, and bleeding."

"I'm on the way, can you move?"

"Yes, but it's painful," I cried.

"Okay, try to get to the front door. I will be there in fifteen minutes to pick you up."

"Please hurry," I cried.

After ending the call with Cordan, I slid off my bed and slowly limped towards the front room so I could wait on him to pick me up. I didn't have to wait too long before I heard Cordan banging on my front door. I opened the door for him and fell right into his arms. Blood was dripping down my legs and my stomach felt like it was being split in half. I saw the fear in Cordan's eyes, but he reacted quickly. He grabbed my keys from off the tray and locked up my house before carrying me to the car.

"Your seats, I'm bleeding, I'm going to mess them up."

"Fuck the seats, I got you."

Cordan laid me back on the passenger seat, hurried to the driver's side and sped out of my driveway.

"Have you tried calling your husband?" Cordan asked as he weaved in and out of the early morning traffic.

"I did, but I can't get him to pick up," I replied emotionally.

"Its okay, you got me."

We pulled up at the hospital twenty minutes later and he rushed me inside the emergency room and demanded that I be seen.

"She's pregnant and she's bleeding," Cordan shouted.

The nurses saw the blood and immediately grabbed a stretcher. They laid me on top of it then rushed me to the back. Cordan was right there with me. I must have lost a lot of damn blood because I started to feel woozy. As they rolled me through the double doors, Cordan held on to my hand.

"Don't leave me please," I mumbled under my breath.

"I'm here baby girl," Cordan reassured me.

Cordan holding my hand and telling me that he was going to be there for me, was the last thing I remembered before I fell into a deep sleep.

JAWAN

I left Alonna's house not accomplishing anything that I had set out to do. All I wanted to do was let her know that no matter what happened between us, I still loved her and really missed my family. Alonna wasn't trying to hear anything I had to say. She had every right to be mad. She really did, but damn! I felt nothing but hate radiating from her when I was around her these days. I cruised through the street and was on my way to head back home. The only thing I could think about was the mess that I had made. I hated lying to my wife, but I was willing to do anything to keep Monay and Alonna with me.

Right now, I felt I had Monay right where I wanted her. She was in love with me and she didn't want to leave me alone, but I knew if I didn't make a decision fast, it wasn't going to be long before Monay started questioning when I was going to make things official with leaving Alonna.

Maybe I was being selfish for trying to hold on to Monay knowing that I was still married to my wife, but I wanted Monay to be mine. Even if she did change her mind and decided that she didn't want to fuck with me anymore, I knew in my heart it was going to be hard to let her go. A nigga was going to be hurt, because I knew the love I had for her was real. I know I may not have been able to give her all of me, but I was willing to give her as much as I could. Leaving my family, I just couldn't do, At least not right now. Maybe if Alonna wouldn't have been pregnant then maybe, just maybe, I would have left my her and given Monay all of me. But even then, I still wasn't too sure.

Alonna had been down for me since day one. She had been my rider and my very first love, leaving her would be a betrayal, I told myself. Sadly, I had already betrayed her once, I had given my heart to another female and I didn't know if things would ever be the same with Alonna and I. If she would have never found out about Monay I would still to this day be sneaking around with her and neither one would have known about the other until I had decided who I really wanted to be with. Right now, shit was in the air and nothing was solid. I saw the pain behind her eyes and I wanted nothing more than to wash it away. She deserved a man who could give her his all, but letting her go to find happiness elsewhere was what I feared. What happened if she met another Drew, a man who didn't love her enough to give her what she deserved and play her for a fool? What happens if she mets another me? Then, where would that leave her? Wanting a man to give his all only for him to tell her he couldn't do it.

I sighed with frustration.

For the first time in years, I finally said a prayer to the man upstairs to shine some light on me and the decision that I needed to make. Apparently, I wasn't strong enough to make the right decision and I needed his assistance. I was a sinner, that's for sure, so praying to him seemed dumb as hell because I felt he wouldn't answer my prayer. But it was worth trying. Anything was better than sitting here and hurting the two women whom I loved.

I know you haven't heard from me in some years, I come to you because I really need your assistance in a matter. I'm in love with another woman and I don't know what to do about this. Should I stay with my wife and kids or should I be with this new love interest? I love both of them and I want to give them both the world, but I'm lost. Please give me some type of sign on what to do.

Amen...

After praying, I hopped out my truck so I could head into the house to shower. Since I was no longer staying with Alonna, I had officially moved into my condo. I wasn't trying to pressure Alonna into letting me move back in if she wasn't ready. I was the one who had fucked our marriage up, so forcing her to do some shit that she wasn't ready to do, wouldn't have been right. I knew eventually when she was ready to forgive me she was going to ask me to move back home. I really missed my kids the most. They were being affected as well. Since Alonna had put me out, I hadn't spoken to them or even seen them.

Going around Alonna's mama wouldn't have been a smart move. I already knew by now that she knew some of the reason why she was keeping her grandkids for Alonna. Her mama never liked me like that, so this was only going to be fire to flame if she found out that I was the true cause of us splitting. The last thing I wanted to do was start a war with her mama. I could be an ignorant ass nigga at times. The only reason why I never laid her mother's smart ass out was because that was Alonna's mother and my kids' grandmother. She was the only bitch I was willing to let get away with certain shit. Anybody else would have been in a ditch some damn where.

Tonight was movie night with Monay. I thought taking her out might take our minds off what we were going through. As soon as I stepped inside my crib, I shot Monay a text to ask her what movie she wanted to see and what time it started. I hopped in the shower and cleaned the grime from earlier that day off of my body. Thirty minutes later, I stepped out of the shower to find that Monay had texted me back with the information.

Apparently, she wanted to watch some scary shit, *Annabelle Comes Home.* I shook my head and chuckled. I texted that I was going to swoop by and pick her up in another hour so we could make the ten p.m. movie. I threw my phone on my bed and headed to my walk in closet to see what I was going to wear. I grabbed a pair of black shorts, a red shirt with Tupac on it, and a pair of my black Nikes. After putting on my clothes, I pulled my dreads back in a low ponytail and sprayed on some cologne. I grabbed my phone and headed out.

I made sure to text Monay to let her know that I was on my way and to be ready. I pulled into traffic and cruised to over to her apartment. I parked beside her car and was just about to get out to knock on the front door, when she came outside. She was looking good as hell. I didn't even want to take my eyes off of her; all I could do was stare.

"Jawan, stop being so weird. Say something if you're gonna stare," Monay joked.

I smiled down at her before telling her she looked beautiful.

She was dressed in a pair of black shorts, a purple top, and a pair of purple and black Air Forces. Her silver hoop earrings dangled from her ears and her hair was pulled into a high bun on top of her head.

"Come on, we have to go. We don't want to be late; you already know the movie is going to be packed," Monay said.

I laughed before heading to my car.

"I don't want to hear about your ass being too scared to

go to bed tonight. I don't know why you want to see that scary ass movie anyway."

Monay clicked her seat belt in and laughed.

"Sounds like you're the one who's scary."

"I'm not the scary one," I joked.

Monay and I laughed and joked the entire ride to the movie theater. It felt good to laugh and talk with her again. It reminded me of the time when we first met and I felt that maybe Monay and I actually had hope to probably getting things on track.

I pulled up at the theater, and just like Monay had predicted, it was packed as fuck. I rode around the parking lot nearly three times before I finally found somewhere to park.

"That's why I told you we needed to get here earlier," Monay muttered under her breath.

"Ughh, I don't want to hear it," I joked.

We hopped out of the truck and headed to the box office to pay for our tickets.

"Do you want some popcorn or something to drink?" I asked her.

She stared over at the line and groaned.

"Fuck the popcorn and drink. It's way too packed; I don't want to miss this damn movie."

I followed Monay to the door that was going to be showing Annebelle and headed inside. We took a seat in the middle and got comfortable. She grabbed my hand as soon as the movie started. Just like I predicted, she screamed through the whole damn movie. When the movie ended she was damn near shaking.

"I told your ass not to see that retarded ass movie. The shit wasn't even scary."

"Bruh, I don't think I can sleep tonight."

I laughed at her ass because she was being serious as hell.

"Baby, calm down. Since you need to be home with your mama, I can always spend the night at your spot."

"Would you really do that?" Monay asked.

"Um, yeah, if you really need me I got you."

"You just don't know how bad I'm going to need you tonight."

I laughed.

"Lil' pussy ass girl."

Monay rolled her eyes and followed me to my truck. After we both gott into my truck and clicked our seatbelts in, I pulled my F150 into traffic and headed back to her crib. As soon as we made it back to Monay's apartment, we headed inside and she went to make sure her mama was good.

"Is Mama Gwen fine?" I asked Monay when she walked back into her bedroom.

"Yes, she's knocked the hell out."

I smiled as she walked over to me. I grabbed her by the waist and sat her down on my lap.

"I really enjoyed tonight," Monay said softly.

"I'm glad. You just don't know how much I've missed you."

"I think I know," Monay replied just before she softly kissed me on my lips.

I held her tightly as I kissed her back. Monay was the one who broke the kiss. The kiss was so deep that I wanted to keep going, but I could tell she wasn't ready. I let her go and she got up and walked away. I watched her as she headed to her closet to find some bed clothes. I pulled off my shoes and laid on top of the bed to get comfortable.

I couldn't tear my eyes away as Monay undressed. Her smooth, milk chocolate skin seemed to glow as the bedroom light hit her just right. I licked my lips as I took in her curves.

"You can look all you want, but you won't to be getting this pussy until you figure out what you're going to do about your situation. I don't want to get myself caught up in none of your bullshit."

I understood what she was saying and I respected it.

"We don't have to fuck until you're ready baby girl," I reassured her. After she turned off the bedroom light, she came and laid down next to me.

I kissed her gently on her lips as I stared down at her.

"I hope you don't plan on staring at me the entire night."

"No, I'm going to bed soon. I just want to make sure you go to bed first, since you scared and all."

Monay chuckled before smacking me.

"Good night Jawan," she replied sleepily.

"Good night, baby girl, I love you," I whispered softly into her ear.

I held her in my arms as I laid their in the dark until sleep finally came for me.

JAWAN

Early The Next Morning...

J woke up the next morning lying next to Monay. She was still knocked the hell out. I grabbed my phone from the nightstand and was shocked to see that I had some missed calls from Alonna and even a text message stating that she was in the hospital. I cursed myself because I forgot I put my phone on silent when Monay and I were in the movies and never took it off.

I hurried to dress and quietly left. As soon as I got in my car, I tried calling Alonna but it went straight to voicemail. I groaned with frustration and sped through traffic towards the hospital that was near our house and hopped out. I didn't know if this was the correct hospital, but this had to be the one that she was at. I rushed to the emergency section and asked if they had someone by the name of Alonna Miles. The nurse nodded her head that she had just been checked into a room.

"I'm her husband, I need to see her now," I demanded the nurse.

The nurse who was an older white woman, told me to follow her. I followed her through the double doors to where Alonna was being kept. As soon as I stepped into her room I noticed she wasn't alone. A man was sitting beside her bed and he was holding her hand. They were in deep conversation. I didn't know who this nigga was; I had never seen him before. He was pecan in complexion and resembled Idris Elba.

"Baby," I said to Alonna.

Alonna turned towards the door and that's when I saw the anger in her eyes; it was all directed at me.

"Is everything okay?" I asked as I walked over to her.

I didn't give a fuck about her attitude, I just wanted to make sure she was okay.

The mystery man stood up and told Alonna that if she needed him, to just call his phone.

"Thanks for being here Cordan, I don't know what I would have done," she replied emotionally.

I watched their exchange and I felt a tinge of jealousy. Whoever this nigga was, he had been here when I hadn't.

After the mystery man named Cordan left, I took a seat next to her bed.

"What happened?"

"Why the fuck are you here? Why show up now?"

"Baby, please I'm sorry. Just tell me what happened."

Tears fell from Alonna's eyes and I knew something bad had happened.

"I lost the baby," Alonna said in a shaky voice.

I felt like the air had been knocked out of my body.

I tried to embrace her in a tight hug, but she hit me and told me to not to touch her.

"Where were you last night? I needed you. I had no one. I ended up having to call my coworker to drive me to the hospital. Please don't tell me you was laid up with that other bitch."

I became quiet as tears fell from my eyes.

I was guilty and Alonna saw right through it.

"Get the fuck out of my face. I hate your ass, Jawan. I just want you to know as soon as they release me, I will be divorcing your bitch ass. We're done. That bitch can have you."

Alonna and I have had plenty of arguments, but she has never talked to me like she was now. She never told me she hated me. I felt like she had taken a knife and had cut my heart right out of my chest. I felt the venom and rage and I knew that Alonna wasn't playing with my ass.

This was it, I had gone too far; I had fucked up and there wasn't any coming back from this. Thoughts of losing my kids and probably never being able to see them like I used to made me feel like the very bitch that she had called me. I had done this to myself.

"Baby, please forgive me. I'm willing to do anything to make this shit right."

Alonna wouldn't even look at me. She was disgusted by me.

"I'm not going to pretend that all of this is my fault. I was angry as hell when I found out I was pregnant. I said a lot of shit that I wish I could take back. You were the one who wanted this baby so much and to know that your ass was the first who was trying to bail out on me for another bitch lets me know you ain't shit, and you can't be trusted."

I lowered my head in shame because she was right. I had choked her out so many times for expressing her anger and frustration about our baby and I was the first one who had left her hanging because of my own selfish needs. I wasn't there like I should have been.

"In a way, it's good that this baby didn't come. We both

are in a fucked up place right now. Neither one of us was emotionally ready for another baby," Alonna whispered.

I grabbed Alonna's hands but she pulled away from me.

"Just leave me alone, Jawan. I don't want to be bothered."

I couldn't leave her in this condition. I couldn't go back to Monay knowing all of what Alonna had went through, and was emotionally going through. I stressed Alonna out the entire time she was pregnant now that the baby was gone, she needed me more than ever. For the first time, I did some shit I never thought I could ever do. I pulled out my phone and called Monay. Her phone rang a few times before she picked up. I could tell that she was still in bed.

"Hey boo, where you at?" Monay asked sleepily.

"Monay, I can't do this anymore."

"What the hell are you talking about? Do what?"

"I can't be with you anymore. I think it's best I set you free."

"What the fuck? What's going on?" Monay cried into the phone.

It broke my heart to hear her cry over the phone. I quickly ended the call and stuck the phone back in my pocket and for the first time, Alonna looked up at me.

"We are going to be okay, I promise," I said to Alonna.

Alonna shook her head.

"It's too late. I think the damage has already been done."

DREW

I felt guilty for being weak and cheating on Desiree
with a chick I had just met, but it had happened
and I couldn't go back to change anything. I should have just
called Kinsley an Uber and that would have saved me from
being in this situation, and I wouldn't be feeling guilty.

As I headed into Desiree's room, the doctor who had been
checking on the status of her coma stopped me.

"Mr. Andrew Wilson?"

"Yes, how is Desiree doing? Is she doing better?"

"I'm sorry sir, her family just left and they have decided
that they are going to pull the plug by the end of the week.
We aren't getting any responses from her. Her chance of
waking up is very slim; I'm sorry."

I stood there in utter disbelief as the doctor walked away.
I couldn't move; I was frozen into place. Tears formed in my
eyes and by the time I was able to walk into Desiree's room, I
was crying like a little bitch. I wasn't able to handle this shit. I
wasn't expecting this to end like this. I still had hope in my
heart that Desiree was going to eventually wake up, but to
know that she wasn't killed me inside. I took a seat beside

Desiree and cried. I didn't know what else to do. To know that I was about to lose the girl I loved fucked me all the way up.

"Baby, if you can hear me, please wake up," I cried.

The beeping of the machines sounded loudly in my ear as I embraced Desiree in a hug. I pulled away from her and took a seat in a chair by the bed and held her by her hand. I couldn't talk. I was too emotional. All I could do was sit there staring at her and listening to the beeping of the machine. I sat there for almost two hours until I finally got up to leave.

"I love you baby girl," I whispered before kissing Desiree on the forehead and leaving.

I had just gotten in my car when my phone started ringing. I shook my head once I spotted the number. It was Kinsley, the fine ass chick that I had fucked a few nights ago in my car. I didn't bother picking up; instead I sent her to voicemail.

I wasn't in the mood to talk right now. I was deep in my feelings over what the doctor had told me about Desiree and her condition. I didn't want to deal with anymore stress.

Having sex with Kinsley and not wrapping it up opened a whole new set of problems that I wasn't in the mood to deal with. Right now, I could only handle one crisis at a time.

I was half way home when she called back again. I groaned with frustration as I looked down at her number while I sat at the red light. I was going to send her to voicemail again, but I knew that if I did she was only going to keep calling, so I decided to pick up just to see what she wanted.

"Hey stranger, how are you?" Kinsley asked sweetly.

"Look, I'm not in the mood right about now, I'm going through some things that I need to work out. I'm going to have to hit you back later," I replied rudely.

I didn't even give her time to respond before I hung up on

her. I threw my phone on the passenger seat and headed home.

A Few Hours Later...

I didn't know how I was going to come to terms with Desiree's family pulling the plug. I didn't have any rights. I wasn't her husband, only her boyfriend. I sighed with frustration. I needed something to calm me down so I could relax. I grabbed the weed that was sitting at my night stand and decided to roll a blunt. Maybe getting high would take my mind off shit that I couldn't control.

I lit my blunt and took a few puffs as I thought about my life and what I was going to do next. Eventually, I was going to have to move on with my life, but moving on seemed foreign to me. I didn't see myself falling in love with another bitch. Falling in love was painful as hell, and I never wanted to feel this type of pain ever again. I wasn't going to spend the rest of my life alone, but giving another bitch my heart wasn't ever going to happen either.

Thoughts of Kinsley crossed my mind a few times. I had been nasty to her earlier. It wasn't her fault about Desiree's situation; she didn't have anything to do with it. I'm sure she was going through things internally after she sobered up and realized she could have been brutally raped at that party. She was a very pretty girl, and niggas were drawn to that beauty. I know I was.

I didn't want to be bitter, I just needed something to take my mind off of Desiree and Kinsley seemed to be the perfect distraction. The chemistry that we had at the party was so strong, I began to wonder if it was just the alcohol or if it truly was us. I didn't see myself falling in love with her or anything like that, but I didn't mind if we explored each other's body again. I was a man and I had needs. As long as I didn't get too close, I wouldn't get hurt.

After finishing my blunt, I put it out and decided to snort a few lines of coke to really get to the place that I didn't give a fuck about nothing. I didn't want to spend the rest of the night crying about Desiree, the decision had been made. My baby was gone, and she wasn't coming back. When I was done getting high, I laid back on my bed and closed my eyes. The dinging of my phone let me knew that I had a text. I grabbed it and noticed Kinsley had sent me a message.

Kinsley: I hope everything's good. I just wanted to tell you again how appreciative I am of you for saving me at the party the other night. It could have ended badly for me. I really enjoyed our time together. Don't be a stranger, I would love to hang out with you again.

I stared at the message a few times before finally responding.

Drew: You're welcome Kinsley, I wasn't about to let that nigga take advantage of you. I'm sure we could chill with one another soon.

Kinsley: What about later this evening? Will you be busy? You can always come by for a little bit.

I didn't have any plans for later that night. Getting high all day was the only thing I was going to do, but since she had invited me over to chill, I decided that I might as well get out. Sitting home moping wasn't going to change anything.

Drew: Send me your address. I can swing by.

There was no amount of drugs that could make me forget the situation with Desiree, but it did relieve some of the stress I was feeling. I put my drugs away and headed to my bathroom to take care of my hygiene so I could head over to see Kinsley. I made sure to shower, brush my teeth, brush my waves down and trim up my beard. I was finally looking like the old Drew, even though I was hurting inside.

I headed into my room and opened my closet to find something to wear. I wasn't in the mood to dress all fly and shit. I settled for a pair of red cargo shorts and a plain black shirt. I found a pair of my black Air Forces and put them on. I sprayed on a little cologne but didn't bother putting on any jewelry. When I was done getting dressed, I made sure to text Kinsely to let her know that I was on my way. I was just about to head out the house when my phone started ringing.

I picked up when I noticed it was my homeboy Red.

"What up Bruh? I ain't heard from your ass since the party. You good? A nigga told me yesterday that you boxed a nigga out at the party that night."

"Yeah, I had to. Some pussy ass nigga was trying to rape this girl. Everybody was wasted or high and nobody was trying to help her, so I got the nigga off of her."

"Shit, yeah you right about that. Folks were high as hell. Was the girl okay, though?"

"Yeah, she was good, she was a little shaken up. I made sure to get her home safely."

"Well, look at you being the Good Samaritan."

"Well I ain't want to just leave her ass to catch an Uber after she had just went through all that shit."

"I understand," Red stated.

"So what's been up with you? How is Desiree doing?"

When Red said her name, a pain hit me in my chest. I didn't want to talk about it, but I knew I had to talk to someone before I went crazy.

"I went by to check on her today. Her family has decided to pull the plug on her later on this week."

"Damn, I'm sorry Drew. I know you over there hurting. Come on over here and chill with me or I can just come over there. I'm here for you, I know how much you loved that girl."

I stood there staring at my car deciding where I needed to go. Should I go to Red's or to Kinsley's?

"I already smoked a blunt and did a little coke to take the edge off."

"Well we ain't got to get high, I just don't want you over there by yourself."

"I'm going to pull up as soon as I get through checking on Kinsley."

"Who's Kinsley?" Red asked quizzically.

"She's the girl that almost got raped at the party."

Red became silent.

"I know everyone grieves differently but I don't know if you need to be using a bitch to get over Desiree."

"No, I ain't trying to use anyone to get over Desiree. I just want to make sure Kinsley good after the other night."

"Drew, you ain't never cared about no other bitch being good until you met Desiree. I know you partna; just be careful. I don't want you bringing no more pain to yourself or causing anyone else any pain because you don't know how to go through the process of moving on from Desiree."

"Well Red, I'm sure getting high isn't going to help the situation either," I shot at him before ending the call.

I was irritated as hell. I hated I opened up to tell him anything. He was always trying to judge shit, just like when I made the decision to leave Monay and get with Desiree. He had some smart shit to say about that, too.

I hopped in my car and put my phone on silent just in case the nigga tried to call me back. I was trying to deal with losing Desiree the best way I could, but getting high all fucking day wasn't the answer, either.

I pulled up at Kinsley's address thirty minutes later and parked beside her Grey Dodge Dart. This was the last place that she had let me drop her off at. The only difference now was, it wasn't dark and I was able to really get a good picture of what type of environment she was staying in.

This wasn't the hood, but it was a step up from the low income assistance. The apartment complex was well kept and nice looking outside. I stepped out of my car and knocked on her door a few times before it opened.

She was standing there dressed in a pair of red booty shorts and a black top. Her lips were painted with red lipstick and her weave wasn't straight like the night before; this time it was wavy and was down her back. She looked very beautiful; it was hard for me to take my eyes off of her. After she closed the door behind me, I noticed that her apartment was neatly furnished and it smelled fresh and clean.

"Um, I can tell by how you look that you weren't expecting this."

I guess my facial expression must have given me away.

I looked down at her small frame and shook my head.

"You really got a nice looking crib."

"Thanks," she replied as she headed into the kitchen. "Do you want a drink?"

"If you got a beer that will be fine," I told her as I walked around her living room.

There wasn't anything separating her living room from her kitchen so I could still see her when she went to get me a beer. I couldn't tear my eyes away from her, no matter how hard I tried. I watched her as she bent down and grabbed a beer out of the lower part of her fridge. Her shorts were so tight and short that I saw nothing but ass staring back at me. I diverted my eyes from her so she wouldn't know I had been staring when she headed back into the living room to hand me my beer.

I popped open the Bud Light and took a few sips of it

before taking a seat on her pretty, deep purple couch. She took a seat on her purple love seat and lit a cigarette.

"I'm glad you were able to come over. I was waiting on you to call me, but you never did. I thought I was never going to hear from the man who saved me at Red's party."

"I've been going through a lot of shit lately, so it was going to be a minute before I was going to reach out to you."

I guess its good I did make the first move then," she replied as she took a puff of her cigarette.

I nodded my head in agreement.

"So how's the girlfriend doing? I remember you telling me in the car before we fucked that you had one."

I almost choked on my beer because this chick was blunt as hell. She had no fucking filter.

"I didn't come over here to talk about my girl."

Kinsley smirked before crossing her legs over one another.

"Well tell me Drew, why did you come over here?"

I sat my beer down on her coffee table before eyeing her up.

"I came over here to make sure you was good, that's all. I see you're doing fine, so I need to be going."

I was trying to get the fuck up out of there because she was trying to get personal and the last thing I wanted to do was get personal about my life. I shouldn't have come just like Red had told my ass.

I got up to leave but Kinsley blocked my way to the door.

"Look, I'm sorry if I offended you. Sit down, finish your beer. We can talk about something less personal if you want to. My kid is gone with her father and I'm here alone. I invited you over so we could get acquainted with each other. I wanted to get to know the man who saved me, that's it."

"It ain't much to know; I don't want to talk about anything dealing with my relationship."

"Cool, I understand," Kinsley replied.

I took a seat back on the couch and Kinsley sat back down as well.

"So you have a kid?" I asked her.

Kinsley eye's lit up.

"Yes, her name is Kamara. She's five. I love that little girl to the moon and back. Do you have any kids?" Kinsley asked.

"No."

"Do you want any one day?" she asked curiously.

"Yes, I do."

Kinsley cleared her throat and put her cigarette out.

"About the other night, I don't want you to think that I'm some thot who goes around sleeping with random niggas."

I eyed her up, because the thought had crossed my mind.

"See, you just gave me that look, so I know you probably think I'm like that. I'm honestly not. that's why I wanted us to sit down and talk so you could get to know me."

"You don't have to explain yourself to me, but I'm listening."

"I know I don't have to explain anything to you but when I met you that night after you beat that nigga's ass, I felt something. When you looked into my eyes, I don't know. It was like this feeling came over me that I couldn't control. I wanted to get to know you so when you offered me the ride to my house, and when you told me bye, I knew if I didn't do something I wasn't ever going to see you again. I was drunk, yes, but I was still in my right frame of mind to know what I was doing. I wanted to experience sex with someone who made me feel like you did. I've never been so attracted to any man like I am with you. I'm normally not so aggressive, but I wanted to get your attention."

"Well, you definitely got my attention."

"Good," she replied.

I watched her as she stood up and headed to the kitchen.

She came back a few moment's later with a glass filled with juice and liquor. "The question that has been burning in my mind since I first laid eyes on you is, do you feel the same attraction to me?" Kinsley asked boldly as she sat back down on her couch.

"I think you're beautiful, but my heart already belongs to someone."

"I know you say you have someone who you love, but if you want me as much as I want you, then just know that I'm down for whatever. She will never have to know, it would be our little secret."

I cleared my throat and drained the last little bit of my beer.

"The offer still stands when you're ready," Kinsley replied.

"I need to be going."

This time, Kinsley didn't stop me. I walked out of her crib and hopped into my car. I sat there for a few moments and tried to get my thoughts together. It was time to be real with myself.

Yes I was attracted to Kinsley sexually, but my heart still belonged to Desiree. I knew that Kinsley was the one who could take my mind off of the stress that I was experiencing, but for some reason, I felt fucking around with Kinsley would eventually lead to some drama that I didn't want to get caught up in, but temptation was real, and she was slowly drawing me into her web.

DREW

The Next Morning...

The ringing of the phone woke me from my sleep. I grabbed my phone from off the other side of my pillow and picked up.

"Hello," I answered groggily..

"Mr. Andrew Wilson, this is Doctor Colbert."

As soon as I heard Dr. Colbert's voice, I sat up in bed. I was no longer sleepy and was ready to know whatever he had to tell me.

"Desiree just woke up, and her family wanted me to call to let you know."

"What? She's awake?"

"Yes, it's a miracle."

"I'm on my way," I replied before disconnecting the call.

I snatched the covers from over my body and headed straight to the bathroom so I could wash myself up. Tears fell from my eyes but they weren't tears of sadness or frustration, but tears of joy. My baby was finally awake.

She woke up, I just couldn't believe the shit. After I

stepped out of the shower I hurried to brush my teeth and put on some clothes. I decided to wear a pair of khaki shorts, with a lime green shirt, and some white Jordan's. I didn't bother making up my bed or cleaning up the bathroom. I was in a hurry to get over to the hospital to see what condition Desiree was in.

I hopped in my Camaro and hit the gas. I was weaving in and out of traffic but eventually had to slow down when I spotted a cop car sitting on the side of the road. I pulled up at the hospital twenty minutes later and ran inside. As soon as I made it to Desiree's room, I spotted her parents and sister. They were hugging each other. Her sister pulled away and walked over to me.

"My sister is finally up. We are waiting until the doctor lets us in so we can see her. He was talking about letting us go in one at a time. He doesn't want us to overcrowd the room."

"You just don't know how glad I am that she is awake."

"I know it was hard on you. It was hard on us all," her sister replied.

There were chairs outside of her room, but the way my nerves were set up there was no way that I could sit my ass down and wait. I paced the floor while her parents took a seat.

"Drew will you please sit down? You're making me nervous as hell," Desiree's mother Debbie scolded.

I stood and looked over at her with a menacing glare on her face.

"I can't sit down right now, so let me pace in peace."

Debbie shook her head and pressed her lips together, before mumbling something under her breath.

The door finally opened a few moments later, and Dr. Colbert came out.

"Desiree is fully awake, and seems to be doing good as far

as memory. She remembers everything, but the issue that she is having the most trouble remembering is the accident. I'm not too concerned about that because as time goes by, she will start to remember."

"Can we see her, Dr. Colbert?" I asked impatiently.

Debbie cut her eyes at me.

"Sure, but one at a time, I don't want her to get too overwhelmed."

"I want to be the first to see her," Debbie demanded.

This scene reminded me of the night Desiree was first taken to the hospital. I was just about to argue with Debbie yet again, like I had done before, but the vibrating of my phone stopped me. I pulled it from my pocket and walked away when I noticed it was Kinsley calling me.

I wanted to ignore the call but decided I might as well answer it instead of fussing with Debbie's spiteful ass.

"What's up?"

"Nothing much, sitting here thinking about you."

I sighed.

I already knew what Kinsley wanted. She had caught me at a time where I was weak. Fucking her shouldn't have happened but it had. Now that Desiree was finally awake, I was going to have to make sure she never found out what had gone down while she was asleep. I knew she would never forgive me if she found out I had cheated on her with someone.

"It sounds like you are busy, so I'm not going to hold you up. I just was calling to check on you and to see if you had thought about what we talked about yesterday."

"I'm okay, just taking care of some business and I'm about to be around my girl."

"I already know how this works, don't worry, I'm not going to call you back since you are going to be occupied. Like I stated yesterday, whatever we do together, she doesn't have to know. I'm feening for another serving of that dick that you gave me in the car."

I wanted to fight the lust that I was feeling for her, but the shit was hard. She was just so damn fine, and hearing her in my ear talking about how she was feening for me, was making my dick hard.

"I got to go, Kinsley."

"Don't keep me waiting for too long, Drew."

After ending the call, I stood there as I tried to get myself together. It was going to be hard as hell to look Desiree in the eyes knowing that I was lusting over another bitch. The crazy thing about it was that I didn't have any type of control over it.

My body was pulling me towards Kinsley and my heart was pulling me towards Desiree. I was so deep in thought that I didn't hear Desiree's sister Kyla behind me.

"Are you okay, Drew?" Kyla asked with concern.

"Yes, I'm okay. I'm just trying to get myself together."

"I understand. I hope you got yourself under control because Desiree is asking for you."

"Thanks," I told Kyla.

I walked past her and her parents and into Desiree's room. I closed the door softly behind me.

"Desiree?"

"Drew, baby," Desiree cried out hoarsely.

I hurried over to where she was lying down on the bed and embraced her in a hug.

"Baby, I've missed you so much," I cried to her.

We held each other for the longest time. I took a seat beside her bed and held her hand in mine.

"You're here? My parents told me that you came to see me nearly every day."

"Of course I'm here. I love you baby girl, I wasn't going to leave your side until you woke up."

Desiree pulled her hands away from me as the tears fell down her cheeks.

"Shhh, don't cry boo, everything is going to be okay. I'm here now."

I wiped the tears from Desiree's cheeks and kissed her gently on her lips.

I guess the last thing on Desiree's mind was her best friend, Monay, well her use to be best friend, because that's the first person she asked about.

"What have I missed? Have you reached out to Monay? Did she come by to see me?" Desiree asked emotionally.

I cleared my throat and was trying to decide if I should tell her the truth or tell her a lie. I didn't want anything to get her too emotional, she was still fragile.

"I know that look. Don't even think about lying to me. I want the truth, Drew."

I sighed.

"I called her when the doctor gave me the news that you were in a coma. She told me that she wasn't going to come and see you."

Desiree nodded her head slowly.

"I guess she still hates me then."

I didn't say anything because deep down, Desiree already knew the answer.

"I guess I deserve it. We were wrong for what we did, Drew. We really hurt her."

"I know we did baby, but there isn't any going back. We can only move forward."

Desiree wiped the last bit of tears from her cheeks before grabbing my hand.

"Waking up today to find that you stayed the entire process let me know that you are the man for me. I would have been heartbroken if I would have woken up to find out that you had moved on to someone new."

I felt nothing but guilt as she leaned in and kissed me gently on my forehead. I should have told her right then and there that I had fucked up, but I couldn't.

I may have been by Desiree's side the entire time, but that didn't change the fact that I had betrayed her. I had cheated on her with someone else, and now I was trying to figure out how I was going to keep her from finding out. I didn't want to break Desiree's heart, but I had no clue how I was going to fight the chemistry that I had for another woman.

Desiree pulled back from me and stared into my eyes.

"What's wrong, baby? It's like you're holding something back."

The guilt was written all over my face.

I lightly caressed Desiree's cheek and stared into her eyes.

"I'm not holding anything back baby, I'm just happy that you will be coming home soon."

Desiree seemed to be satisfied with my answer and didn't question it.

"I love you so much," she muttered as she wrapped her arms around my neck.

"I love you too," I choked out.

MONAY

$\mathcal{I}$ was beyond hurt. I couldn't believe that Jawan had called me and ended things so coldly. Just when I thought we had an understanding, he ends things without even explaining himself. I had been so hurt and depressed that I didn't even bother by going to work last night.

My mind was fucked all the way up, and I didn't know when I was going to get myself together. I was in love with this man, and he had broken my heart twice. If there was a button to turn off my love for him, I would have gladly pushed that bitch. I didn't want to go through the process of getting over a broken heart, but as I laid in bed, I knew that was part of being human. We were meant to feel emotions, no matter if they were good or bad.

The ringing of my phone was the only thing that made me stop crying. An ounce of hope soared through my body. Maybe it was Jawan calling me telling me that he was sorry, and he didn't mean anything that he had said. I grabbed my phone and the tears started back falling as soon as I saw that it was my coworker Jasele calling me. I wanted to ignore it, but Jasele never called my phone, so I knew it had to be about something important.

"Hello," I said tearfully into the phone.

"Monay, are you okay? You didn't show up to work last night. I just wanted to make sure you're good."

I became quiet as I tried to hold back the tears.

"I'm alive if that's what you want to know, but I feel like dying."

"Monnnaay, are you crying?"

I sniffled.

"What happened? Talk to me."

I needed to talk to someone. I needed to get this shit off of my chest.

"He broke up with me..."

"Your boyfriend?"

"Yes. He decided to work things out with his wife."

Jasele grew quiet.

"I know you're in pain boo, but you are going to get through this. I wish I would have known about this earlier, I would have warned you to be careful."

"I know, but it's too late for that."

"I'm here for you if you need me. You don't have to go through this alone."

"I know. Thanks Jasele."

"Are you coming in tonight?"

"Yes, I have to. I need the money. Last night my emotions were all over the place; there was no way I would have been able to come in so I stayed home."

"I understand. We will talk when I see you at work."

"Okay," I muttered before hanging up the phone.

I buried my face in my pillow and laid there until I heard my mama call out my name.

I got off my bed and wiped the tears from my eyes. I couldn't lay here all day knowing I had a sick mother in the next room. I was going to have to suck this shit up and take care of her before I could figure out about my own feelings, and what I was going to do about the whole Jawan situation.

I walked into my mama's room to find her lying in bed. Her hair was scattered across her head and she smelled like pee.

"Mama, I'm sorry. I was in my room resting. Let me get you out these wet clothes and give you a bath."

"Okay," she replied weakly.

I ran Mama a warm bath and helped her in the tub. While she was bathing, I made sure to strip her bed so I could wash her sheets. I was glad that I had listened to the doctors when they told me to put a waterproof mattress pad under her bed sheet so she wouldn't mess up her mattress. I threw out the soiled pee pad under the bed and put her sheets and comforter set in the washer, then turned it on.

I hurried back to the bathroom to find that Mama was still bathing herself.

"Good job, Mama."

"I told you I could bathe myself," she stated proudly.

"Yeah, you sure did," I chuckled.

When her bath was done, and after her teeth and hair were brushed, I helped her into the living room so she could sit down until her sheets were finished washing and drying.

I grabbed an Ensure out of the fridge and popped it opened for her.

"Drink this because I already know you are not going to eat if I cook."

"I hate these too," my mama complained.

"I'm not going to fuss with you this morning lady. Drink this or I will cook."

Mama sighed before snatching the chocolate shake out my hand.

"I guess I might as well drink this," she muttered under her breath.

I took a seat next to her and leaned back on the couch.

"Is everything okay?" she asked gently.

I shook my head no.

"What's wrong, Monay?"

"Everything," I said softly.

"Talk to me, then."

I took a deep breath.

"I feel dumb as hell, and let's not forget, weak as hell."

"Nope, I don't want to hear you talk like that in this damn house."

"Sorry," I muttered.

"Yah, you better me. Now tell me what's going on."

"Jawan called and broke it off with me. Apparently, his love was fake from the jump. He chose his wife over me."

As the tears fell down my cheeks my mama put her shake down and held me.

"I'm here for you. I know you may be hurting now, but give it time, you will get through this. You're a strong woman Monay. This is just a minor set back. I know you love Jawan, but sometimes the people we love can't give us what we need. I don't want you settling for less, because you deserve someone who can give you their all. It's time you understand that Jawan can't give you his all if he has a wife. His obligations are somewhere else; you have to learn to accept that for what it is. You can't change it, no matter how much you want to. I don't want you putting your life on hold waiting on him either. Go out, experience life Monay. Do things that you never got a chance to do. Before I die, I want you emotionally happy."

I couldn't hold back the pain I was feeling. I cried for the love I had for Jawan, and I cried because the love I always wanted from my mother, I was finally getting, only for it to be cut short. Life wasn't fair, this I understood, but why couldn't it give me a fucking break and for once let me be happy?

"I think it's time you heard the truth."

"The truth about what?" I asked her.

"Your father."

I froze. I never knew much about my father. The only thing my mama told me was that my father left when I was a baby. I was so young back then that I didn't have any remembrance of him anyway.

Mama cleared her throat and took a deep breath before she finally told her story.

"Your father and I were very much in love, at least I was in love with him. I met him when I was nineteen and he was twenty-nine. We met in Kay Jewelers. I was instantly attracted to him from the moment we laid eyes on one another. He was very good looking, and was a gentleman. He was there looking for a necklace for his wife's birthday, so I helped him find one that he liked. We talked for a little while and he told me a little about himself. When he passed me his phone number, I was in disbelief. Back then I didn't know anything about side bitches or none of that.

I was young, dumb, and naive. He told me so many sweet lies about how he was going to leave his wife and be with me, but everything changed when he found out I was pregnant with you. He cut me completely off and it was like he disappeared."

"Yeah, he disappeared. He moved to another town, Mama."

She nodded.

"He wanted to get as far away from me as he could, so that his wife never found out."

I shook my head.

"He never called, or wrote, or anything. I never heard

from him again. He just up and walked away like I meant nothing to him. You look so much like him. I wanted to forget him, but every time I looked at you, I saw him."

"I'm sorry that you had to go through that."

"Yeah, me too. But it's life. Shit happens. The only thing I want to happen when I die is for you to be happy and for you to actually get to know your father. Just like we finally got to know each other. You deserve to have that closure from both of your parents."

"I tried reaching out to him some years back when I was a teenager."

My mama sighed.

"He may not have responded because his children are close in age with you. They should be fully grown now. Just try to reach out to him again, and I want this to be a promise. When I die, I want you to really want to try to get to know your father. If he turns you away, at least you tried, baby girl."

"I don't even know if he is going to want to get to know me."

"Always expect the unexpected, baby. Now, let us find something to watch on TV before you have to go to work tonight."

I rolled my eyes.

"Let me guess, you want the Lifetime channel."

"You already know," my mama chuckled.

I flipped the TV on and laid down on my Mama's lap as we watched a movie in silence.

MONAY

$\mathscr{I}$ woke up to the sound of my mama snoring. I checked the time and knew if I didn't get my ass ready, I was going to be late. I left Mama on the couch asleep as I headed into my room to take a shower before work. After I was done showering, I hurried to put on my work clothes for that night. I pulled my hair back into a tight bun, dabbed a little lipstick on my lips, and put a little eyeliner under my eyes. I was trying to fix myself up but there was no amount of makeup to hide the pain that was displayed on my face.

After I was done getting dressed, I headed to the living room to wake my mama up.

"Ma, I'm heading to work. You need to get up so I can help you get into bed."

Mama groaned but stood up and held on to me as we headed into her bedroom. I sat her down on her bed as she started to undress.

"I know you're tired, but let me find you something comfortable to wear."

I found mama a t-shirt and a pair of pajama pants, and

helped her put them on. When she was dressed, I put her under the covers and placed a kiss on her forehead.

"Okay mama, I'm going to see you in the morning. Whatever you do..."

"I already know, don't get out of bed."

"Right."

I handed her the remote to her TV and told her to have a good night. I was just about to head out the door when she grabbed me by my arm.

"I love you, Monay."

"Awwww, I love you too, mama," I whispered back.

I headed out of her room and out of the house. I pulled out my phone just to see if Jawan had texted or called me while I was asleep. My heart instantly sank when he wasn't anywhere to be found. I shoved the phone into my purse and hopped into my car so I could head to work.

As soon as I pulled up at my job and stepped through the double doors, Jasele was sitting there waiting on me. She embraced me in a tight hug and passed me a small gift that was wrapped to perfection.

"What's this?" I asked Jasele curiously.

"Well, sometimes we all want to feel appreciated and loved. I thought you needed cheering up, so I got you something small. Open it girl," Jasele demanded playfully.

I opened the perfectly wrapped box and stood there in utter disbelief when I spotted a pretty silver necklace that was heart shaped with Survivor written inside.

"I was at a jewelry store and just happen to see it, and I thought about you."

"Thank you so much. I love it," I replied emotionally.

"Good, now let me put it on you."

I stood still as Jasele took the necklace from me and placed it around my neck.

"It looks good on you, just like it was made for you. When

times get hard, I want you to look down at your neck and know that you are a survivor, and you can and will get through anything."

"Thanks Jasele."

"You're welcome," Jasele replied.

The ringing of the phone reminded us both that we were at work. I brushed my tears away and got to work with booking rooms, while she dealt with customers who weren't satisfied with the service of the hotel.

When everything had settled, Jasele and I munched on snack foods and watched YouTube on the computer. Even though I was still upset about the Jawan situation, knowing that my mama and my coworker actually cared about me and my feelings ,really made me feel somewhat better.

Some people had to pull their selves out of the pain that they were experiencing. In my case, I had two women who were trying to make the pain that I was going through a whole lot less painful.

We were in the middle of watching a YouTube video when the front doors swooshed open and I spotted a cop walking towards us. He was a white man, medium in height, with a buzz cut and looked to be in his early thirties.

"Aww, shit, here comes the damn law," Jasele muttered before cutting off the YouTube video we had been engrossed in.

"Good evening ladies, I'm here to see a Ms. Monay Hayes."

"That's me," I informed the officers slowly.

The officer introduced himself as Officer Murray.

"What can I do for you, Officer Murray?" I asked quizzically.

"I'm sorry to be the one to tell you this, but your mother Gwen Hayes has passed away at home."

I couldn't speak and I couldn't move. I stood there frozen into place.

"Ma'am, the police and ambulance responded as soon as we could."

Tears fell from my eyes as I let out a screeching scream.

No, it couldn't be real. My mama couldn't be dead. I had just seen her a few hours ago and she was just fine. She was okay, she was watching TV.

I screamed, and screamed, and cried loudly.

I fell to the floor. Jasele fell to the floor next to me, and held me in her arms.

"I'm here, Monay."

"Noooooo!" I yelled.

I don't know how long it took for me to get myself together, but once I had, the officer finally started answering the many questions that had been running through my mind.

"A neighbor called the cops because your mother wouldn't answer the phone or come to the door. The police were the first to respond on the scene to do a wellness check to make sure she was okay. Her body was found in a bedroom on the floor. The coroner has her body and is checking to find the cause of death."

I cried even harder because I knew it was my fault. I knew my mama had cancer and she was very weak and frail.

If she was found on the floor, that only meant one thing. She must have fallen trying to get out of the bed. I preached to her on numerous occasions to never get out of the bed if I wasn't there, but she always insisted she could handle herself. I shouldn't have come to work tonight. She was dead all because of me, I told myself.

"I'm sorry for your loss. Give it twenty fours and the coroner should be done with her body. I suggest you contact the funeral home of your choice as well," the officer stated sadly.

"Okay, I will," I muttered.

I looked back at Jasele and she embraced me in a tight hug.

"Go and take care of your business, I can run things here. Remember Monay, you're a survivor. You're going to get through this, she whispered into my ear."

I only hoped that Jasele was right because I sure didn't know if was I going to be strong enough to get through the heartache that I was going through.

MONAY

I left my job and hopped in my car. I sat in my Honda for the longest time before I was able to leave the hotel parking lot. All I wanted to do was get home to see for myself if Mama was truly dead. I pulled up at my apartment twenty minutes later and parked alongside a police car. The ambulance was packing up to leave and the police had the house blocked where I couldn't get in.

"I live here," I cried out as I tried to push the officer aside.

The police finally let me through and I ran inside my mother's bedroom to find it empty. I fell to the floor as an officer came to my rescue.

"I'm sorry for your loss, ma'am."

I weakly stood up on shaky feet and headed into the living room to take a seat. I sat there for thirty minutes and watched as everyone packed up to leave.

I was in deep thought until I heard someone call out my name. I looked up and spotted my mom's best friend, Judy, standing in the doorway. Even though Judy and I didn't always get along because I always blamed her for helping my mama get drugs, seeing her again brought back old memories. I could tell that Judy had been crying.

"What are you doing here? I thought you were in rehab?"

"I was, but I'm out now. I came home today, and came by to see your mama but no one would could come to the door. I got worried and called the police, and that's when I found out that she had died."

Judy wrapped her arms around me and held me as we both cried. I pulled away from her first and stared up at her. For the first time, Judy appeared to be healthy. She had picked up weight, and she had grown her hair out. She was dressed in a pair of torn up jeans with a red shirt, and a pair of red sneakers.

"I never got to say goodbye," Judy cried.

I was speechless, and my mind was still processing what had happened. Judy and I took a seat next to one another on the couch. We talked until the house became empty and everyone had gone home.

"I'm supposed to go to the morgue tomorrow to view the body and I have to make funeral arrangements," I informed Judy.

"If you need any help, feel free to come by my house and let me know."

"I will."

After Judy left, I sat there on the couch as the tears continued to fall from my eyes. Life just wasn't fair.

The Next Morning

Making funeral arrangements was something I wasn't prepared to do. My mama didn't have a will and never talked about where she wanted to be buried. We didn't attend church, so finding the perfect funeral home was all on me. I decided to choose a black owned funeral home that was located down the road from my house. I called and got all of the information that I needed. I wanted to give her a nice burial, but money was tight, and she didn't have a life insurance policy. The only thing I could afford was cremation with a small ceremony.

When the coroner called, I made sure to let him know to transport my mama's body to the funeral home that I had chosen down the road from my house. Guilt consumed my body when I was informed that Mama died from falling in her bedroom and hitting her head. If I would have never gone to work, she would still have been alive. I didn't think I was ever going to get over the pain that I had endured. My mama was gone, and now I had no one. I was all alone.

I stood up off the couch and headed into the bathroom so I could shower. I stood in the shower for an hour crying as the hot water washed over my tired body. After getting out of the shower, I threw on some comfortable clothes and went into my bedroom and sat on my bed. I grabbed my phone that was sitting next to me and noticed that I had two missed calls from Jasele. I touched the necklace that was still around my neck and knew that Jasele was right. I was going through a tough time, but I was going to get through this. I had to.

The only person I wanted to talk to was Jawan. I needed him to be here with me. I wanted to call him, but I wasn't sure if he was even going to pick up. I debated if I should call as I stared down at his number. What was I going to do? What would I do if I called and he had me blocked? What was I going to do if he didn't want to hear from me? I took a deep breath and called him anyway. It was just a risk I was willing to take.

Jawan picked up on the first ring.

"Monay?"

I froze because I didn't think he would answer my call. I didn't know if he would even recognize my number. I thought he may have deleted it.

"Monay, is everything okay?"

"Jawan I need you. My mama is dead."

JAWAN

J had been thinking about Monay since I ended things with her. I knew I had broken her heart, and I hated myself for it. I promised her that I would always be there for her and I fucked around and turned my back on her. I was caught in the middle of showing my loyalty to my wife or to the girl I had come to love.

At the time, I felt my wife needed me the most. Alonna was still suffering emotionally from the loss of our child. She was devastated and I made sure to stay by her side every step of the way so she knew that she didn't have to go through this pain by herself. That was our baby, and I was very much affected by losing the child as she was. Alonna and I both blamed ourselves. We had been so stupid and dumb the entire pregnancy, and now the baby was gone and their wasn't anything we could do about it but move on and try to live with the pain.

I was back living in my house with my wife and kids. Things were far from perfect, but at least I had my family back. There wasn't anything that Alonna could do to stop the love that I had for Monay. It was too late, Monay had a piece of my heart just like she had. As soon as Alonna made it home from the hospita,l she started talking about us packing up our things and moving to Savannah. I already knew what she was doing. She wanted to save our marriage. She wanted a fresh start. She wanted to forget all the hurt and pain that she had endured in Atlanta, Georgia. My business was here, the girl I loved was here. I didn't want to move. I didn't want to start over. I loved the life that I had here and the money I made here. When I expressed this to her, she accused me of not leaving because I didn't want to leave Monay. She was partly right; I didn't deny the accusation because it was true.

Monay was all I could think about, and now she was all I wanted. I didn't know just how much I needed her until it was time for me to cut her off. Every night when I laid with Alonna and held her close to me, I secretly wished that it was Monay. Every time my phone rang I wanted it to be Monay calling me, but today something changed. All the hoping and praying that Monay would reach out to me had finally come to an end, and she finally called.

I was inside the grocery store with my wife Alonna and the kids. When I saw Monay's number pop up I froze. I had erased her number from my phone but her number was saved inside my mind, and when I saw it, it was like some-thing in my heart lit up. I hurried to pick up and told Alonna it was a business call and walked off from her and the kids. I didn't give a fuck if Alonna grew suspicious or not, I had to hear Monay's voice; I had to make sure she was okay.

But when I heard her broken voice in my ear, sadness filled my entire body. Monay was broken and it was all my fault. The last thing I was expecting her to tell me was that her mother had passed.

All I heard was that she needed me and then the line went dead. I wasn't able to call her back because the kids came to find me to tell me they were getting ready to check out. I followed the kids to the cash register and paid for the food that Alonna had stashed in the bucket for dinner that night.

"What's wrong, baby? It looks like you have a lot on your mind."

There was no way I could tell Alonna the truth; she would literally lose her shit right at the grocery store. Instead, I told her that I had to make a quick run when I got home.

She already knew what I meant when I said I had to make a run, that meant drug talk and she wasn't going to question me on it because she didn't want to know details.

After paying for the groceries, we headed to the car with the girls singing and skipping. The kids seemed to be very happy that me and Alonna managed to finally be a family again. I knew my kids needed me, and I was planning on always remaining in their life, even if Alonna and I didn't make it as husband and wife.

"How long are you going to be gone on this run?" Alonna asked as soon as we got into the car.

"I don't really know Alonna, it's going to be late though."

"I guess I will save you a plate for you to eat tonight," Alonna commented.

"Yes, that will work," I assured her.

As soon as we got home and after I had helped Alonna put up the groceies, I kissed her on the cheek and told her I would see her later. The kids gave me a big hug and wanted to know why I was leaving and was I going to be home to eat with them. I gave them both a hug and told them that I was going to be home as soon as I could.

They ran off and went back to their rooms to play.

I didn't waste any time with grabbing my keys and heading out to the car. I wanted to get my ass over to Monay's house while I could.

When I pulled up twenty five minutes later, I sat in the

car as I tried to get myself together emotionally. It had been a few days since I had last seen her. She called me so I knew she was going through some things emotionally and needed me. I wanted to be there for her, and give her the support that she needed. I also wanted to give her the love that she truly deserved.

I stepped out of my car and knocked on her door a few times before it opened. When our eyes connected, my heart began to race and my mouth went dry. I didn't know what to say or do. I felt dumb as hell just staring at her. She stepped aside to let me in. I only took a few steps into her house before I turned around to face her.

I saw the tears falling from her eyes and I knew exactly what I needed to do. Maybe right now, words weren't what she needed; she needed comforting instead. I embraced her in a tight hug as she sobbed on my chest.

"There you go beautiful, get it all out. I'm here now," I whispered to her.

I held her until Monay's body finally stopped vibrating and her tears dried up.

I wiped the remainder of tears from her cheeks and stared down at her.

"I'm sorry about your mama, baby girl."

Monay didn't speak, she only nodded her head.

"I know this is hard for you, but I want you to know that I'm here for you."

"I'm shocked that you came. I didn't think I would ever see you again."

"I'm sorry, Monay. I just did what I thought was right. My wife lost the baby, she needed me."

"But I needed you too. You promised me Jawan," Monay cried out.

"I know I did, and I'm sorry for breaking that promise.

Do you know that you haven't been the only one suffering from the choices I made? I'm suffering just like you."

"No, I highly doubt it, You got everything you want. You got your perfect wife, your kids, and what do I get? My mama is gone, I'm all alone. All I have is a piece of a job with no money to bury my mama."

"I may have all that but I'm missing you. I can't go another day without hearing your voice, or seeing you."

I shook my head.

"You were doing just fine before I called."

"No I wasn't Monay, I was dying inside. Look, I want to turn this shit around. I'm willing to do anything to prove how much I really love you. I know I have fucked up your trust, but baby, I need you in my life. I didn't know how much you affected me until Alonna suggested we move from here and start over in Savannah. I couldn't bring myself to leave Atlanta because I knew I would never see you again."

"What about your wife? Are you going to leave her this time? I'm not putting my life on hold waiting for you to leave her. Either you're going to be with me, or you're going to be with her."

"I want you, Monay."

"Prove it."

"You say you don't have the money you need for your mama's funeral. Name the fucking price and I will handle it. I will make sure she has a nice funeral, just like you would have done if you were able to."

Monay squinted her eyes at me but finally let down her guard to name the price that she wanted to spend for her mama's coffin and her burial.

"Is this going to be a big funeral?" Jawan asked.

"No. My mama didn't have any family living. It has always been me and her, and her best friend Judy. There's no point in doing a ceremony and only Judy, me, and you going."

"Right, I agree."

"We can just purchase a casket, a tombstone, and do the viewing before actually burying her," Monay replied emotionally.

"Have you found out which funeral home you're going to use?" I asked Monay quizzically.

"Yes, it's a black owned funeral home up the road that I want to use."

"Okay, cool."

"Can you come with me to get things situated?" Monay asked curiously.

"Yes, I'm not ever leaving you again."

JAWAN

I spent the rest of the evening helping Monay get things situated. I knew she was stressed, but I did everything I could to make things easy for her. The last thing I wanted her to do was worry about money. I was willing to dish out whatever she needed. I wasn't one of them dope boys that blew all the money I made. I was a smart ass nigga, and invested my money as well as stashed a lot of it away for a rainy day and for my girls' college funds.

When we were done with the arrangements, it was time for us to get something to eat. It was close to six in the evening and I was starving.

"Are you ready to eat something?"

"No," Monay, said tiredly.

"Well, you got to eat baby girl."

Monay sighed.

"I'm taking you out to a nice dinner."

"You don't have to do all of that. I honestly don't want to be around anyone right now."

"I understand boo, but going back home only to be depressed doesn't sound pleasant either."

"Okay fine. I will go to dinner, but I'm going home afterwards."

"You don't want to stay at the condo with me for a few days?"

Monay looked over at me like I had lost my mind.

"Why are you looking like that?" I asked her quizzically.

"Do you remember what happened last time I was over there?"

"You ain't got to worry about my wife, she already knows I'm going to be gone for the day."

Monay shook her head.

"I don't know about going to your crib, I got a bad feeling about it."

I sighed before telling her if she didn't want to come over to my crib then I was going to come over to hers. She didn't seem to have a problem with that idea at all.

"Where do you want to go eat?" I asked Monay as I cruised through the Atlanta streets.

"It doesn't matter to me. I ain't hungry, anyway."

I shook my head at her as I pulled up at the nearest Sonny's and hopped out. I grabbed Monay's hand and we headed inside. We took a seat in the back booth and were given menus.

It didn't take me long to figure out what I wanted, but Monay held her menu and didn't speak for over ten minutes.

"Um, have you decided what you want?"

"Ughh, don't rush me, I'm trying to decide."

I chuckled.

"My bad, baby girl."

"Yeah, whatever," Monay replied.

"Have you decided when you want to actually have her buried?"

Monay sighed.

"No, I haven't given much thought to it. All I know is it's going to be in the next few days."

After placing our orders, Monay and I found ourselves talking about our future and what she was going to do now since her mama was gone.

"Do you plan on keeping the apartment, or will you be looking for something else?" I asked Monay curiously.

Monay became quiet as she sipped on her iced tea.

"I want to move and get another apartment. That apartment has some bad memories, as well as good memories before she passed."

"I understand. Well, if you're serious about moving, I can find you something."

Monay cleared her throat.

"I don't have the type of money you have to afford anything you pick out for me. You must have forgotten that I'm low income."

"Not anymore, because I'm going to take care of you," I explained to her.

Monay shook her head.

"I'm not looking for a man to take care of me, I don't need your help. I will manage."

"I want to help, you're my girl. I'm not gonna have you living in the hood. I got you, boo. All you gotta do is continue to go to school when school starts back in the fall and work, but only if you want to. I'm not going to stop you from doing whatever you want to do with your life, I just want to know that you're safe."

Monay seemed like she was in a deep thought.

I grabbed her by her hand.

"You can trust me. I promise you, you can."

"You sure are making a lot of promises."

"And I plan on keeping them."

"We will see," Monay replied suspiciously.

I understood that it was going to take time for Monay to trust me, but I had all the time in the world to make shit up to her. Being without her really opened my eyes to see that what we had wasn't just a deep infatuation, but I was in love with her young ass and I couldn't live without her.

Cutting her off was like cutting a part of myself off. Some type of way, I was going to come clean to Alonna. If I knew Alonna like I thought I did, this wasn't going to go well with her. She was going to be super pissed, and I was risking everything for Monay. I only hoped that I wasn't about to make a mistake that I wouldn't be able to change later in the future. I wasn't just about to hurt Alonna, but my kids as well. My kids only knew me and their mama. They didn't know anything about Monay.

I knew if they met her they would love her because she was a sweet person, but the question was, would Alonna even let me be in the girls' lives? So many questions and not enough answers.

Monay must have noticed the stress on my face.

"You're thinking about your family?"

"Yes."

Monay became quiet.

"I can't make everyone happy. I have to choose. No more trying to keep ya'll both. It's not possible. Neither one of ya'll are side bitch material. Y'all are more than that. I love both of ya'll, but..."

"But what."

"You're the one I can't see myself being without."

Monay bit down on her bottom lip as she processed what I had just told her.

"Don't be playing with me, Jawan. I hope you're serious this time."

"I am, baby girl."

The food came a few moments later and I dug in. Monay

took a few bites of her bbq and potato salad and sat her fork down.

"You've got to eat more than that, Monay."

"I can't. I'm just so hurt right now. You just don't know how shitty I felt when I found out about mama."

"Talk to me," I softly said to her.

Monay took a deep breath.

"It felt like my entire world had ended when you broke up with me over the phone. The last conversation I had with my mama, she held me while I cried and told me that she wanted me to be happy. She told me the story of my father and how they met, and how she wanted me to find him when she died."

As I stared at the girl who had stolen my heart, my chest grew tight.

"I promised my mama I would contact my father and try to get to know him. Honestly, I don't even know if he would even want to get to know me."

"All you can do is try," I stated gently.

"I know. It's just, I wish she was still here. You just don't know all the shit that my mama put me through growing up, and then when she finally gets herself together she leaves me. I feel like everything is my damn fault. I knew I shouldn't have left her alone by herself with her being sick. She knew not to get out of the bed Jawan, I don't know why she got out that bed," Monay stated emotionally.

"You didn't know Monay, you couldn't protect her 24/7."

Monay shook her head.

"I could have done better, I should have just gotten a CNA to come to the house and sit with her. But she fussed so much about how she didn't want anyone taking care of her but me."

"It's going to be okay Monay. Your mama is still alive in

your heart. The funeral will be in a few days, and I'm coming along to be your support system."

"Thanks Jawan for dropping everything and being here for me."

"That's what a nigga do when he loves you."

Monay nodded her head in agreement.

"My mama's best friend was the one who found her. She is all I have left of my mama. Judy and Mama were very close. They used to get high together, but once mama got clean, Judy decided to get clean, too. I know she's hurting too, we both are. Judy ain't the same crack head she was when her and mama used to get high together. Getting off of drugs changed her. I can tell just by how she acted when she came over last night."

"That's good, baby. It's good that she stopped in time to live her life."

"You're right. Too bad my mom won't be able to live hers."

DREW

*D*esiree had been awake for three days, and today was going to be the day she finally came home. The doctor was satisfied with her progress and felt she was able to be released. Everyone's prayers had been answered, mine included. I pulled up to the hospital to pick her up. I had spoken to Desiree's parents earlier that morning and they made plans to have a small surprise party to welcome her back home. I was all for this idea and thought it would be good for her.

I pulled up at the rear of the hospital and jogged inside. Her discharge paperwork had been signed and she was waiting on me. I kissed her gently on her lips as I wheeled her out with her wheelchair. I helped her in the car and a nurse came outside to retrieve the wheel chair before I pulled off.

Desiree seemed to glow and I knew it had everything to do with her being happy to be alive, and to be going back home.

"Where are we going?" Desiree asked as I made a left

when I was supposed to have made a right if we were going home.

"We're making a detour right quick."

Desiree didn't object, she just leaned back in her seat and seemed to enjoy the ride. We pulled up at her parents' house thirty minutes later. Her eyes grew wide and I smiled.

"Yeah, surprise."

"My mama had something to do with this I bet."

"Yep, something like that."

"I hope she didn't give you a hard time while I was in a coma."

"You have no idea."

"Yeah, she is like that at times. I never had the chance to tell her about you."

"No worries, at least your sister knew about me. She was the one who filled them in."

"I'm sure Kyla enjoyed every moment of having to tell my parents about my love life," Desiree joked.

I hopped out of the car and helped Desiree out from the passenger side. I didn't bother by knocking on the door, I opened the door and we were both met with her parents, her sister Kyla, her husband and her little girl Morgan.

"Surprise!" everyone screamed.

Desiree beamed as everyone welcomed her with a hug and open arms. I sat back and observed as Desiree interacted with her parents.

"Okay everyone, come sit down so we can eat," Debbie ordered.

I followed Desiree into the kitchen and noticed that the food had already been set out. Debbie prepared and went all out. She cooked a ham, greens, cornbread, yams, and for dessert, chocolate cake.

I took a seat by Desiree and held her hand as her, father Stan, said grace.

We dug in after grace was said. Everyone made small talk, but it wasn't long before Debbie and Stan directed their questions toward me. They were trying to get to know me. I didn't have an issue about any of it; it was time that her parents got to know me as the man that Desiree was in love with. Stan seemed to be impressed and eventually, Debbie's entire attitude changed when she learned that I was a street nigga.

"Don't you get my baby caught up in no dope boy shit," Debbie stated seriously.

"No disrespect Mrs. Debbie, but I can protect Desiree."

Debbie seemed to finally gain some respect for me and dropped the cold demeanor. I guess she realized exactly who she was fucking with and didn't want any smoke. After Desiree's parents were finished questioning me, they started on Kyla and her husband, Requan.

My phone started vibrating in my pocket. I pulled it out, and saw that it was Kinsley calling me. I could have ignored her call but I wanted to talk to her. She really had a nigga debating about fucking with her again.

It had been hard as hell to stay away from her ass these past three days that Desiree was awake. I didn't know what was wrong with me. Desiree had everything I needed, but I still felt something was missing. I kissed Desiree on her lips and told her I was going to step outside on the porch because I had a business call. I headed out the backdoor that was close by the kitchen and sat down in a chair on their patio.

"What up," I said into the phone.

"Hey Drew, I'm just thinking about you."

I smirked.

"Oh really?"

"Hell yeah, I wanna see you again. You still ain't gave me my answer."

"I'm around my girl right about now."

"Uggghhh, so I guess what we did was a one time thing then. I might as well lose your number," Kinsley commented.

This was the time right here for me to tell her to leave me alone, that I was in love with my girl, and I wasn't about to cheat on her. This was the time to cut everything off, feelings included. I told myself that it was just a one time thing. She had caught me at a time that I was weak and high off drugs and I didn't enjoy the pussy or head. But as much as my mind told me to cut Kinsley off because I had something good, my lustful thoughts won.

I wanted her, at least one more time, I told myself. One more time to sample the pussy just to see if it was as good as it was the night we were drunk and high. Maybe it was the drugs that had her pussy feeling so damn good. Her pussy could have been wack and her head could have been horrible. I needed one more time with Kinsley. When we were done, I was going to change my number and be completely faithful and loyal to Desiree.

I took a deep breath before I finally gave Kinsley the answer she had been waiting for.

"I'm going to fuck you one more time, but after this time, we got to cut this off. I love my girl."

"Baby, when you get this pussy again, you're going to forget about your girl."

Her warning didn't make me cautious; instead, it excited me which made me want her even more. She was enticing me and she knew it.

"I'm coming through tonight, so be ready."

"Oh, trust and believe, I'm going to be waiting butt ass naked for you. Do you remember how to get over here?"

"Yes, I got it saved in my phone."

"Cool."

"I'ma see you around eight tonight."

"Okay."

I was so deep in conversation I didn't even know that I wasn't alone. I ended the call and slid my phone back into my pocket. I turned around to head in the house and that's when I spotted Desiree standing there with tears rolling down her face.

I don't know how much she had heard, but she must have heard enough, because she was crying.

"How could you?" she cried to me.

"Baby, let me explain".

Desiree shook her head at me.

"I don't want to hear it. I was laid up in the fucking hospital and here you were fucking another bitch? Really Drew? How could you do some shit like that to me? I was fighting for my life, and you wasted no time to find another bitch to replace me."

Desiree laughed as the tears fell down her face.

"I guess this what I get for falling in love with my best friend's nigga. You did me the same way you did her. I thought we had something real, but now I see we don't."

Pain and guilt filled my heart.

"I can't stand the sight of you right now," Desiree hissed.

I tried to grab Desiree so I could talk to her, but she quickly told me to not touch her.

"I'm going back inside, I think you need to leave."

I watched as Desiree walked back into the house. I stood there for the longest time. Had I lost Desiree already? Was there any coming back after this? Could she ever forgive me? Was our love strong enough to get through the lust that I had for another woman? I had so many questions running through my mind with no answers to any of them.

MONAY

*B*eing around Jawan and having him help me get through the death of my mother was unexpected. I thought I had lost him forever. I wanted to trust him, and for things to go back to how they were when we first met, but I just didn't want to open up and have him dump me off like I was some piece of trash. I couldn't help that I loved him, but I wasn't about to be his fool.

All the shit he was saying about taking care of me while I finished school, finding me an apartment all sounded good, but none of it moved me. I was tired of hearing his sweet promises. I wanted to see some action. I wanted him to prove to me that he wanted me. I didn't want to hear anymore lies, I was tired of him selling me dreams.

After eating dinner at Sonny's, we ended up back at my place. We were laid out on my living room couch watching TV and feeding each other ice cream. For the first time, I laughed and joked around with him.

"That's the Monay I know and I've missed. I like you better when you're happy."

"I just haven't had anything to be happy about."

"Soon you will have everything to be happy about, you will see."

I rolled my eyes at his statement and turned my head towards the TV. He held me in his arms until I fell into a deep sleep. I don't know how long I slept, but I woke up to him kissing on me. I looked around and noticed that we were not in the living room but we were in my bed.

"What are you doing?" I asked Jawan sleepily.

"I'm giving you all of me."

I was half asleep but as soon as he started taking off my clothes, I was wide awake. Having sex wasn't the answer, but my body had been feening for his since the day he had made love to me with his mouth. This was going to be our first time going all the way and a bitch was nervous. I felt like my heart was going to beat out of my chest. He must have felt the mixed emotions that I was feeling because he quickly told me to calm down.

"I got you baby, you're going to enjoy it."

I already knew I was going to enjoy the dick but what I didn't know was how I was going to act afterwards. I was already crazy in love, I didn't want to lose all sense of myself if and when he went back to his family. I was going to be pissed and salty. Instead of opening up to let him in, I pushed him off of me.

He knew all too well what was bugging me.

"Baby, I'm not leaving you after this. It's just going to be you and me. That's it. Trust me."

I wanted to run when told me to trust him. I've trusted him since day one, and my heart had been broken twice so far. I didn't think I could come back from the third heart-break. My brain was fuzzy and I could barely think clearly. He had a hold on me already and I hadn't even gotten the dick, yet.

I couldn't fight the chemistry or the love that I had for

him. I wanted to detach my emotions from the physical act, but that shit was too hard for me. All I could do was lean back on the bed and let him have his way with me. I wanted Jawan and he wanted me. That was all that mattered.

I moaned as his lips met mine. He slid his tongue into my hungry mouth and kissed me like I was the only one he ever wanted. He pulled away from me and continued to take off my clothes until I was completely naked. When my jeans and t-shirt were on the floor, he snatched off my thong and I removed my bra. He kissed and sucked on each of my erect nipples as he placed his hand between my thighs. I whimpered as he slid a finger into my wetness.

"Damn, you so fucking wet," he whispered into my ear.

He placed feather light kisses from my face all the way towards my honey box. When he dipped his tongue into my love nest, I gripped the bed sheets as he licked and sucked on my clit, which I immediately brought me to my peak. My legs shook as he licked up my sweet nectar. He came up for air and kissed me before pulling away to remove his own clothes.

I was mesmerized by his body.He was fit and he looked good enough to eat. His long dreads were halfway down his back and his pretty eyes made me weak. I had always been sexually attracted to light skinned men, and Jawan was the perfect complexion.

"Are you ready for this pipe?" Jawan asked.

I nodded my head to let him know that I was ready for whatever.

"Relax baby girl, I'm not going to hurt you."

I wrapped my legs around him as he slid into my love tunnel.

I gasped.

"Shiiit," he groaned as he pushed deeper into me.

He slid his tongue into my mouth to hush my cries as he filled my walls with dick. I scratched up his back as he move inside me.

"Your shit so damn tight," he choked out.

I wasn't in pain, but I was crying because of the joy that I was feeling inside. We wasn't fucking and he wasn't being rough with me, he was actually making love to me. He took deep slow strokes as he looked down at me. We kissed and he sucked on my neck as he passionately showed me with his body just how he felt about me.

I gasped when he picked me up and sat me on top of him. I straddled him and slid his long pipe inside of me. He rubbed his hands over my erect nipples as I slow grinded on his dick. I placed my hand on his chest as I took my time and rode his pole. I gasped and cried out his name when he started beating my pussy up, as he held me with his hands.

"I'm about to cum," I cried out.

"I'm cumming with you baby," Jawan groaned.

He smacked my ass a few times before slamming his dick into me one last time and spilling his seed deep into my love tunnel.

When we were done, neither one of us could move. All we could do was lie there and bask in our loving making. He pulled me close to him and held me in his arms as he rubbed his hands through my hair.

"Did you enjoy, baby girl?" Jawan asked softly into my ear.

"Yes, I did. It was everything that I had been dreaming about."

"Good," he replied.

I was just about to close my eyes but as soon as he touched my sweet spot I knew that I wasn't going to be getting much sleep that night.

I turned to face him and he took that time to get on top of

me. I opened myself up to him. I moaned his name as soon as he slid his magic stick into my tight folds.

"I'm never leaving you ever," Jawan said to me before placing his lips on mine.

ALONNA

*I*t was eleven p.m and this nigga still hadn't brought his light skinned ass home. I had been calling him since eight, and he had yet to respond. Me and the kids had eaten and they were in bed. I picked up my phone one last time to call him and all it did was ring for a few times and then I was sent to voicemail. I was pissed because I knew he was on some fuck shit.

He claimed he had to take care of business but he never went hours without calling or texting me back. It didn't matter how busy he was, he always picked up his phone. I left my bedroom and headed into my kitchen. I grabbed his plate out the microwave and trashed the bitch. I knew he wasn't going to be home anytime soon. He was tied up right now, and there was only person who I knew probably had his attention. My blood was boiling and I was ready to fuck some shit up. I thought I had gotten my husband back, but apparently that bitch still had her claws in him.

I went back into my bedroom to roll a blunt. After smoking half of it, I put it out and headed to the shower to wash up for bed. I was trying to do anything to take my mind off of Jawan and his fuck shit. Crying wasn't going to solve shit; it wasn't going to bring my husband back home. My mind told me to forget his ass and end the marriage because he didn't want me.

Cordan was the only nigga who had been there for me and he wasn't even my husband. He had stood by my side through my miscarriage, and had been calling and messaging me to make sure that I was healing properly. He truly cared, and I didn't have any history or kids with this man.

He could have easily turned his back on me but he hadn't. He owed me nothing, but seemed to give me everything that I expected Jawan to give me. I didn't want to give up on my marriage and Cordan understood that. He also told me that if my marriage could be saved, then I should do whatever I could to save it and promised to never touch me again while I worked on my marriage. So far, he had kept his word. He said he wanted me happy and I believed him. I wanted to be happy with my husband and I didn't want to give him up, not ever.

We had both cheated. We were both even. It was time he stopped playing with my heart and we got back to working on our marriage, because we had both fucked up, but it wasn't over until one of us was dead. I was ready to start over, but apparently he wasn't ready. I wasn't about to sit around and let him continue to fuck another bitch behind my back. It was time he chose either me or Monay.

After getting out the shower, I hurried to get dressed. I picked up my phone to call him one last time but decided not to once I saw a message from Cordan.

Cordan: Is everything okay? I haven't heard from you today.

Alonna: I'm about to lose my fucking mind, Jawan has been gone since early this afternoon, I already know he on some fuck shit and with that other bitch.

Cordan: Calm down, please, don't do nothing stupid.

Alonna: Oh, I'm about to locate his fucking phone because I'm about to pull up on his ass.

Cordan: And what you going to do if he's with her? Then what?

Alonna: I want him to choose Cordan, I'm his wife, I'm not coming second to no bitch. I want him to look me in the eye and I want him to tell me he is choosing her. I want him to see just how illogical and dumb he looks. There is no way he is going to throw away ten years of our marriage for another bitch who he just met.

Cordan: I'm coming with you.

Alonna: No, I'm going to handle things myself. Thanks for always being here for me. I need to do this myself. I need closure.

Cordan: Okay, be safe.

Alonna: I will. Talk later.

I grabbed a pair of grey shorts, a white top, and put on my white Air Forces. I was ready to drag this bitch's ass because obviously, they thought I was something to play with.

After I was dressed and my hair was brushed down, I went into the kids' room. I picked up three year old, Aliana, and carried her to the car in her pajamas. She was still knocked the fuck out as I put her in her car seat. I went back in the house and picked up my two year old Arianna and strapped her in her car seat by her sister. After the kids were secured, I locked the front door behind me and jogged back to my car.

It didn't make any damn sense that I had to take my kids with me, but they were sleep. I wasn't about to let them stop me from dragging a bitch tonight.

As soon as I started my car Cardi B's *Pull Up* started playing. I cut the music down because I ain't want to wake the kids. I hurried to track Jawan's phone and put my GPS on as

I rapped to the song. I replayed it a few times before I finally pulled up at the house that Jawan's phone had said he was at. I parked right up beside Jawan's truck. I looked around for a few moments before I stepped out of my car. I knew instantly that I was in the hood.

As soon I stepped out my car, I spotted a big ass brick. I grabbed the brick off the ground that was lying beside a big tree that Jawan was parked under. The brick was heavy as fuck, but I managed to pick it up and throw that bitch right through Jawan's front window.

The sound of breaking glass filled the quiet night. The apartment that I was at was pitch black, but I knew his ass was in there with that bitch. I felt it in my soul. I walked my ass up to her door and started pounding for someone to come and open it up. I pounded forever before the lights started turning on in the house. When that door opened and I spotted her ass, I wasted no time by popping her in the face.

I could tell she had been in the bed because she ain't hardly have any clothes on, but a tank top and a thong.

"Bitch!" she screamed.

This bitch was going to find out that she was fucking with the wrong bitch. I might have an education and wasn't from the hood, but I knew how to handle myself.

"Where's my husband, bitch?" I asked her as I punched her in the face with my knee. She fell back and I grabbed her ass and slammed her against the wall, knocking down pictures and anything that was hanging on for decoration. She head butted me and punched me in the face a few times before kicking me in the stomach.

"You done broke into the wrong house, bitch!" she shouted just before she punched me in the nose.

Blood spilled from my nose, but I wasn't about to let that shit stop me from whooping her ass. I charged at her and pushed her down on the floor. I punched her ass in the face a good five times, before I was lifted off of her.

"What the fuck is going on? Alonna, what are you doing here?"

"Nigga get your ass off of me. You told me you was out handling business, but here you are, over here fucking this hoe!" I screamed.

Monay didn't say shit. I glanced over at her and then back at him.

"I'm tired of the fucking lies Jawan, I got the fucking kids in the damn car. You're trying to play me like I'm some dumb bitch. Have you forgotten that I've been with you long enough to know when you're running game? We have kids, we're married. We just lost a child and what do you do? You're going to throw ten years away for this bitch who is living in the fucking hood?" I screamed at his dumb ass.

Monay cut in and tried to say something but I told that bitch to shut the fuck up before I hurt her young ass.

"Since you have both of us in the same room, you can't lie any fucking more. You can't tell this hoe one thing, and tell me something else!" I yelled.

"Bitch, I didn't even know shit about you. I'm not a hoe," Monay spat.

I chuckled evilly.

"Bitch, you're a fucking hoe, because now you know and you're still fucking my husband. Look at you. You're half naked, and look at Jawan. He's wearing boxers. Stay out of this conversation Monay, I'm not talking to your ass."

I turned my attention back to the man who always promised me that he would love me, and never hurt me.

"Now I want to know what you're going to do Jawan. Enlighten me and Monay. Who are you going to be with? Are you really going to leave your family for a bitch you just met? Are you really going to do some shit like this?"

The whole time I was screaming at the top of my lungs, and all Jawan did was is stare at me. He didn't say shit. I finally took a deep breath to calm myself down.

"I think it's time that both of ya'll know the truth. I'm not going to keep lying to either one of you. Neither one of ya'll deserve the shit. Alonna, I first want to tell you how sorry I am. We've been holding each other down since high school. I married you, had all my kids by you, and wanted to spend the rest of my life with you. I fucked up this marriage and I can own up to the shit. I want you to know that I will always love you and I plan on being in my kids' lives, but it's time for you to know that I can't do this shit anymore. I'm tired of all the lies I've been telling to keep you and Monay. I love you Alonna, but the love we had when we first got married isn't there anymore. Don't stand there like you don't know. Don't look at me like you ain't felt the distance. I stayed so long because of the kids and because of my loyalty to you, but even you said when you first got pregnant that we wanted separate things and you felt we had outgrown each other.

Back then, I was in denial, but when Monay came into my life, I knew that what I wanted with Monay, I could never have with you anymore. We have outgrown one another Alonna, and it's time for you to accept it for what it is."

I didn't know how to react. I had to have heard this nigga wrong. There was no way that he had just picked Monay over me.

"You can keep the house, the car ,all that shit. I will even continue to pay your way through nursing school and I will pay child support."

I felt like my heart had been ripped from out of my chest as what he said began to sink in.

He was leaving me.

Monay stood there and I looked over at her. Her mouth was wide open in astonishment. I guess she wasn't expecting for him to have chosen her, neither. Jawan must have lost his mind. He wasn't thinking any of this shit through.

He tried to touch me and I right hooked him in the jaw. He was lucky that I didn't have a weapon on me because I swear if I did, I would have used it on his dumb ass.

"You know what, I'm not going to beg you to be with me if you don't want to be. If that little bitch is what you want then gon' right on ahead Jawan. But she will never be me," I spat angrily.

Jawan shook his head.

"That's the point of me getting her Alonna. I don't want another you."

Hearing him say some shit like that hurt me to my soul.

I charged at him but Monay stepped in and punched me in the eye. I cried out in pain and swung on her ass. I grabbed her by her hair and started beating her in her face. Jawan broke us up and demanded me to leave.

Monay and I were both bloody from fighting. Blood dripped from my mouth and I wiped it away. I was near tears, but I refused to let them fall.

"I can tell that you don't even know me, Jawan, because if you did, you would know that you just fucked over the wrong bitch. I hope she was worth it, because I promise you that you will never have a happy day with that bitch as long as I have breath in my body."

I walked out of the house slamming the door behind me. I hopped in my car and was glad that the girls were still asleep. I pulled out of Monay's yard and headed back home. There was no time for tears; my mama didn't raise a weak bitch. I wasn't about to cry over no nigga.

Monay thought she had taken my nigga from me and he actually thought he was about to have a happily ever after. They both were slow in the brain if they thought this. When

I got done with the both of them, they were going to wish they never fucked with me.

To Be continued….
Part 3 coming soon...

Connect With Me On Social Media
JOIN MY READER'S GROUP: https://www.facebook.com/groups/636779069802790/ This group is where I will be showing sneak peeks, doing book giveaways, and have discussions about my books.

FACEBOOK PERSONAL PAGE:
https://www.facebook.com/profile.php?id=100011411930304

FACEBOOK AUTHOR PAGE: https://www.facebook.com/Shanice-B-The-Author-1699513303656006/

TWITTER: @ShaniceB24

GOODREADS: https://www.goodreads.com/author/show/15039114.Shanice_B_

BOOKS BY SHANICE B.

In Love With An A-Town Thug Part 1

Endless Hood Love (Standalone)

Feenin' For That Dope Dick

No One Has To Know: A Secret Worth Keeping

Meet Me In My Bedroom: A Collection Of Erotic Love Stories
(Volume 1 & 2)

All I Need Is You: A Christmas Love Story

I Wish You Were My Boo: A Tragic Love Story

Your Love Got Me Shook: A Novella

Married To The Dekalb County Bully

Love, I Thought You Had My Back: An Urban Romance

All I Ever Wanted Was You: A Twisted Love Story (Part 1 &2)

He Loves The Savage In Me: A Twisted Love Affair (Part 1 &2)

Kiss Me Where It Hurts (Part 1-3)

ABOUT THE AUTHOR

Shanice B was born and raised in Georgia. At the age of nine years old, she discovered her love for reading and writing. At the age of ten, she wrote her first short story and read it in front of her classmates who fell in love with her wild imagination. After graduating high school, Shanice decided to pursue her career in Early Childhood Education. After giving birth to her son, Shanice decided it was time to pick up her pen and get back to what she loved the most.

She is the author of 21 books and is widely known for her bestselling four-part series titled Who's Between the Sheets: Married to a Cheater. Shanice still resides in Georgia where she is a devoted, nurturing, and caring mother of her six-year-old son.

CPSIA information can be obtained
at www.ICGtesting.com
Printed in the USA
LVHW041650161019
634411LV00002B/356/P